# AFFECTION

## Emotion Series

Cynthia L. Evans

BLUEPRINT PRESS
INTERNATIONALE

ISBN
978-1-961117-21-1 (Paperback)
978-1-961117-22-8 (eBook)
978-1-961117-20-4 (Hardcover)

# AFFECTION

*Emotion Series*

# Table of Contents

# 1

# CHAPTER

"It's too hot!" I breathed with a heavy breath. It was the dead of winter and somehow, I was sweating. My heart was beating fast and my hands were shaking. "The heat isn't up too high, is it?" I thought as I turned to get out of bed. When my feet touched the cool floor, I realized there definitely wasn't an issue with the thermostat. It was me! I quickly sat back down and thought about what happened this past year. I'd just been promoted to Health Information Manager at Riley Children's Hospital at the age of 25 and I was ecstatic. I have a great 3-bedroom 2 bath Ranch house in a wonderful neighborhood in the suburbs of Indianapolis so, no complaints there. I'm a single African American woman and I thought I was pretty but, average looking. A native of Indiana and one of three girls I was raised to take make sure I could take care of myself. Dependence on a man was not an option. From a young age, I attended a great private school and had the best resources available to me from day one. My dad a manager and my mother a medical assistant made sure to instill the importance of a good education. You were not allowed to become a bum and do nothing. If you wanted to be successful, you had to work hard and get a good education. Thanks to my parents we lived in a safe neighborhood, attended the best schools and were all successful women today. I mean, I don't blame them. I'd be proud too. We never did drugs, we're not alcoholics, and none of us have a criminal record.

I knew that the reason for all this even being possible was because of the love and power of God. Our parents came from humble beginnings and they didn't have much growing up. My father one of ten and my mother one of six both knew what it meant to struggle, and they didn't want that for their children. They fought hard and defied a stereotype that has been over our culture for far too long. They are educated, live in a nice neighborhood, and have great careers. It's because of them I am where I am now. They raised us in the church and made sure we understood that with God all things were possible. Of course, like most children I forgot that sometimes but, I always came back to God. Growing up we were close, and we are still close. I go home from time to time and especially for the holidays. I love my parents so much and I appreciate all that they've done for me. That's why it was sad for me to move three hours away. However, my parents wouldn't hear about me turning down this opportunity and encouraged me to go. I know for a fact that without them and the grace of God I wouldn't be here today. Despite all this my subconscious was trying to tell me something. I started to shake again from worry. What could make me wake up so hot and sweaty in the dead of winter? I didn't know but, what I did know was that I didn't have time for this. I had to get up for work soon. It was currently two in the morning so; I made sure to pray for peace and went back to sleep.

Six hours later I woke up feeling much better and started to get ready for work. I slowly pulled the blankets away and shivered when the cold air hit my skin. My feet hit the cold floor again for the second time in eight hours. "I really need to start wearing socks to bed during the winter." I thought as I made my way to the bathroom. Located to the left of my room was a door that led into my bathroom suite. I quickly made my way inside. I decided to decorate it with a roman theme in mind and was very happy with the results. I love the color of brass fixtures so; the faucets and door handles in my house were all brass. The bathroom floor was a reddish-brown tile with a strip of jewels in the middle. The countertop was made of grey marble and double sinks. My tub was a special soaking and whirlpool design. It was perfect for long days on my feet at work. I also had a two-person shower that featured the tile in a very special design with matching smaller tile for the shower floor. It had two showerheads on opposite sides so, you could shower in peace without disturbing the other person. Plants and vases were put in distinct sections to pull off a garden feel, and I loved it. This wasn't here when I first bought the house of course. I had to have renovations done to reflect my taste and I was very happy with how it turned out.

I quickly took my shower, brushed my teeth and walked into my walk-in closet. The closet was connected to my bedroom on the right side of the room and had a cherry wood door. Inside it was 140 sq. ft. and it was my second favorite room in the house. It had yellow paint on the walls and cherry wood drawers were located on the right side. In the middle were four separate closet rods a top each other and they had my work clothes on one and regular clothes on the other. On the left side of the room was my shoe rack and held up to 100 pair of shoes. I didn't have anywhere near that many pairs but, my friend who customized and made the closet for me suggested it since I planned on getting married one day. I decided on a white blouse outfit with matching black pants that had white stripes flowing from hip to toe. For my shoes, I went with a nice pair of black boots and faced the mirror on the back of the door to see how I looked. I liked what I saw and headed back into the bathroom to do my hair. I am proud to say that my hair is natural so, it doesn't take me as long to do it as it did when it was permed. I took the water spray bottle out of the sink drawer sprayed my whole head. My hair is long and hangs down to my shoulders. It took quite a long time to train it to do this through a process called stretching. Being tender headed I didn't like the process that much but, it was worth the results. Once I was finished I took my hair curling cream, rubbed it in my hands and proceeded to apply it to my hair. It always felt good to do this part in the morning. It was kind of like getting a massage every day. I put my hair band on my head to push my hair back out of my face and I was ready to go eat breakfast.

The rest of the house except for the kitchen had a medium toned carpet covering the floor and the kitchen was covered with a cherry wood artificial floor. It was a great floor. It was easy to clean, and I never had to worry about waxing it. Once I was in the kitchen I went straight to the fridge and opened the freezer door. I wanted some pancakes and some eggs this morning. I'd just started making my eggs when my phone rang. I picked it up and saw it was my mother. I didn't answer the phone. I knew she was just calling to remind me about the family get together coming up in a couple of weeks. I told her I'd already be coming but, I knew she just wanted a head count. I put the phone back down and returned my attention to my eggs. My kitchen followed the same theme as my bathroom looking like a roman kitchen. My friend renovated it for me as well and made sure that when you walked in you felt like you were in Italy. With brass kitchen fixtures, sandstone colored marble counter tops, cherry wood floors and stainless-steel appliances it really felt prestigious. It was an average size kitchen but, with an open concept design it felt bigger. It opened into my living room space so, it was perfect for entertaining. The style of the house is a ranch and that really helps with keeping your heating and cooling costs low. On top of that I have a full finished basement and a laundry room located next to the two-car garage. Yea, I loved my house. Once I finished eating I was finally ready to go to work and walked into the garage. I pushed the garage door opener and got inside my 2016 navy blue Chevy Cruze. It was January and only 50 degrees outside so, I didn't really need to turn the heat on. It was a nice a mild winter and I was only wearing a light sweater over my blouse. While I backed out onto the street I turned on the radio and listened to the traffic report. I never usually had a problem getting to work but, I liked to check it every morning just in case. It was only a 15-min commute for me and it was a pleasurable drive. This was mainly due to how the city was set up and I've never complained about it. However, I should've thought about what caused that uneasiness last night. Since everything was going great in my life I just pushed it into the back of mind. I figured I was just nervous in my new position. It wouldn't be until later tonight when I would learn what my body was trying to tell me.

Walking into work I felt a sense of pride. Thanks to the affordable care act the last 5 years with medical records have been about switching from paper to electronic. It created tons of jobs in my field and I was in high demand before I even graduated from college. I got a job at Riley Children's Hospital and I oversaw the Health Information Department and made sure that the medical records were processed accurately, safely, and had no breaches in our computer system. I'd just been promoted after working as a record release specialist for 3 years. I am very new to this position but, I love the challenge. I never have a dull day. The hospital walls were decorated with cartoon pics of animals and bright colors that led you to different parts of the hospital. It felt like you stepped into a children's storybook. Each color went to a specific department and it proved to be very effective in such a huge facility. With it being winter outside it made you feel very happy and like a child again when you walked through the doors. I made my way to the bank of elevators and noticed the crowd of people waiting to get on. Of course, many had coffee in their hands. "The miracle of the morning" I called it even though I couldn't drink it myself. I still could appreciate the benefits it gave to others in the morning though. When the doors opened indicating to get on I made my way in with the rest of the group. I'm pretty sure we looked like a herd of cattle by all accounts. Buttons were pushed, numbers lit up and we began our ascent. The floor numbers sounded off as it climbed its way up till it reached my floor number six.

When I stepped off the elevator a feeling of "freedom" ran through me and I earnestly walked to my office. Walking into the department my coworkers greeted me cheerfully everyday despite it being early in the morning. I personally am not a morning person. To be honest if I didn't have to I wouldn't be coming to work earlier than 10 am. The Health Information Department consisted of 14 employees and they were all in charge of making sure the EMR which stood for Electronic Medical Record system ran soundly. We put in the patient's medical records that came down in paper form and we would scan them in the EMR. Whenever a patient came into the hospital a chart would be created in the system and everything would be put in electronically. Sometimes when a doctor ordered an ultrasound or an EKG the results would come back in paper form and we were the ones in charge of scanning them into the EMR. This also went for lab results or chemo that was done in the hospital too. Another part of the HIM department was to make sure that all the information was attainable and put in correctly. If that was not done major errors would happen and the hospital would be liable for any accidents that would occur. The department wasn't really decorated. It was pretty plain. The walls were white, and the floor was covered in blue carpet. There were ten cubicles that were put together in the middle of the room and that allowed for some privacy. On three of the walls were paper charts that were waiting to be shipped out to hospitals storage facility. Our goal was to be completely electronic in two years so, we have slowly been shipping them out for the last three years. Once they were all gone there would no longer be any paper charts here at the hospital. On the plus side, we did have a nice view of the city from the one east side of the department so, none of us complained about the lack of decorations. Matter of fact, my team was great, and we worked extremely well together. We didn't argue or have any childish issues between one another. It was a great place to work and I looked forward to coming in every day. Basically, I wouldn't trade them in for anything. It's far too difficult to find hard working people that you not only got along with but, also loved their jobs. As I made my way to my office I walked past the break room and the assistant manager as well as my friend Shania popped her head from behind the door.

"Morning Sareya!" Shania called from the break room.

"Morning Lauren, how are you this morning?" I asked as I walked past her to make myself some tea.

"I'm good. Today is going to be an easy week huh?" she said after taking a swig of her coffee. Yea, she was one of them.

"Why don't you ever drink tea Shania? It's a lot better for you? Besides, I don't think you need any caffeine. You're perky enough for all of us in the morning." I laughed as I poured hot water into my mug and then added my lemon tea bag.

"Wow! Am I really that cheerful?"

"Yes, dreadfully so. You know it's a little after 8 am right?" I asked her as I poured a spoonful of sugar into my mug.

"Yes."

"You know I don't fully wake up till 10 am right?" I asked.

"Yes." She answered as she moved closer to me.

"Then why in the world do you insist on talking to me in your chipper voice even though you know it annoys me?"

"Because it annoys you." She said as she began to laugh.

"It's way too early for this." I said as I walked out of the break room.

"Well, I have to do something. You have been ignoring my requests to hang out for the last two years."

She followed me out of the break room and continued to follow me all the way into my office. My office wasn't big, but it wasn't too small either. It was decorated tastefully with white walls, a dark wooded desk, a leather desk chair, and plain blue comfortable seats for my guests. I had one file cabinet that sat behind me and they held the important documents I would need for meetings and training purposes. On the wall hung my college degree and, on my desk, was a picture of my family. My parents and my two sisters. I had a nice view of the east side of the city so, just like everyone else I didn't complain about the lack of decoration. Honestly, it suited me perfectly.

"I'm sorry. I know we haven't hung out much but, I was working my butt off trying to get this promotion. It should be nice a slow here now that we have the new EMR running smoothly. We won't have any meetings for at least a week and since our boss Eli is out of the office we won't have any side projects we have to do either."

Our boss was out for a week due to an outpatient surgery but thankfully, it was nothing serious. See, I really liked my boss and we were great friends. We went to high school together and I had no idea we would end up at the same medical facility only a couple of hours from our hometown. I really lucked out on that one. He was the Director over the HIM department and he got the positon after working there two years. Just like me the previous person retired, and they needed new blood to come in. One that was familiar with the new computer systems and had knowledge of the new laws that were in place. It also helped that he had a bachelor's degree in HIM and had his certification as an RHIA. That's Eli. He always went big or he went home. I wanted my Associates degree and my certification as an RHIT because I wanted to get out into the workforce sooner and move down to Indianapolis. Which thankfully actually happened. We never dated but, many people in high school and college thought that we did. He asked me out once but, I told him that I didn't feel that way towards him. I saw him as a great friend and I didn't want to ruin it. He respected my decision and never asked me out again. Suddenly realizing I was still standing at the door of my office I walked behind my desk and set my tea next to my keyboard. As I sat down my seat creaked and I logged into my computer.

"Well, since you're just going to ignore me I'm going to go back to my desk. I had a crazy weekend thanks for asking!" she said as she gave me a smirk.

"I'm so sorry Shania. I didn't sleep very well last night." Shania's eyes lit up. She quickly closed my door, made a quick U-turn and took a seat in my chair.

"OOOO, what happened Sareya? Did you finally go out this weekend?"

No, I did not"

"Don't lie to me Sareya. If you went out with a guy you can tell me."

"I didn't go out with anyone Lauren!" I yelled as I got frustrated with her.

"See, this is what I'm talking about! All you ever do is work, work, and work! Ever since two years ago whenever I invited you to go out with me you would always say no. You were always saying something about men getting in the way of our fun or something like that. How was that even possible?"

"What!" Did she really just say that? It is way too early in the morning for this type of conversation and now I was irritated at the fact that she would bring it up so easily. She did have a point though. Two years ago, I did stop hanging out with her and I have been working a lot. Can I really be looked at as a criminal for that? That is the very reason I got this promotion and I don't regret the hard work I put in here. Still, would it really hurt to go out every occasionally, now that I am a manager?

"That's what you said Sareya! Do you really have something against men or are you just avoiding me?" Lauren said as she began to feel disheartened. She was right. I have turned her down a lot and yet she kept asking me anyway. I really need to treat her better than this. She is a good friend after all.

"No, I didn't go out this weekend but, I promise I'll go out with you sometime this week ok. You're right. It has been long time and I really could use some fun." Especially, after what happened last night.

"Really! She said as she jumped out of her chair and clapped her hands together. OOOOOOO, I'm so excited I'll let you know what day we can go ok. You just made my day. I'm leaving before you change your mind. See you later!" She yelled and walked out of my office.

That's Lauren for you, all 5 ft. 2 in and 130 lbs. of her. She was thick by society's standards and was in great shape. She exercised three times a week and ate healthy for the most part. On the weekends, she splurged by eating fast food and didn't drink pop. Counting carbs and fats were never her thing so, she mainly stuck to just maintaining a healthy diet. She used to run track in high school and got good grades. Thanks to her hard work she got a scholarship to IU running track and got her degree in Information Systems. She was one of four children which consisted of two girls and two boys. I never met her family since they live an hour away but, she said that they were somewhat close. Her parents are kind of controlling and they didn't want her to move far away but, when she got this job offer she took it and left. She said if it hadn't been for that she'd probably still be there doing whatever they wanted her to do. I commended her for being so brave to make that move on her own. I know other people who would never have dreamed of moving far away from their families. However, I was not one of those people.

We started are careers here at Riley's around the same time and we hit it off right away. She was a very good friend and we are the same age. She would always dress so cute and after seeing my clothes a month after starting here she decided to help me dress nicer too. I was a tomboy growing up, so my closet consisted of mostly jeans and t-shirts when I first arrived. That simply wouldn't do for Shania. She insisted on taking me to the mall and other various stores to help me (as she put it) save my wardrobe. By the time she was finished with me I had a slew of dresses, work outfits, shoes, boots, hair accessories, jewelry, and even a new pair of glasses. She felt it was time for me to update those as well. All the new clothes in my closet were all thanks to her and the design of my house was largely her input as well. She had learned that I loved the roman designs and helped me figure out how to make my house represent the culture in a tasteful way. She accomplished this all within my budget and thanks to my friend who did the renovations I did save a ton of money. I didn't know why she took up a career in HIT instead of fashion or home decorating but, I assume it had something to do with wanting to make sure she had a steady paycheck. Her fear was to never be without money so; I'm basing my rationing on that theory.

We used to go hang out all the time. We would go dancing and sometimes even go to some of the local bars but, I was never much of a drinker. I loved to dance. However, I didn't like doing the clubs too much. All they did was gyrate and that was not actual dancing to me. Shania did so, I took it upon myself to teach her different forms of that I learn since my freshman year of high school. I started studying dance in high school and went on to even minor in it in college so, my concept of dancing was totally different than what everyone else was doing in the clubs now a days. I preferred to do some the ballroom style dances like swing, foxtrot, the waltz and I also loved to go to the stepper halls. That's right a sister has major skills. I found dance to come easy to me and studied ballet, jazz, tap, and modern dance. Thanks to the years of dancing my body was is very toned. I'm 5 ft. 1 in and weigh 120 lbs. I'm kind of built like Rochelle Aytes with a little more muscle. I'm a little darker complected and with a lot of stretching my natural hair hangs all the way to my shoulders. I have big brown almond shaped eyes and nice full lips like Kerry Washington and thanks to Shania I have plenty of makeup to help accent them whenever we went out. Lessons to teach me how to do my makeup were taught by her as well and now I can do it with ease in a pinch. Hanging out with her was fun and safe. Neither one of us were partiers if you will but, we were young and liked to have ourselves a good time. I enjoyed every moment of it until... No, I can't think about that now. It's all in the past and it's time for me to move on. I forgave myself and God forgave me too. There's no sense in dwelling on something I can't change.

The screen lit up with my favorite quote as my background picture that read "As I look back over my life, I realize that every time I thought I was being rejected from something good, I was actually being redirected to something good". Man, was that true. Nobody is perfect but, it can be hard to realize that it all will work out for my good sometimes. That's why I had this on my background. I also had a calendar on my desk that read inspirational quotes or verses that was given to me from my mother. I appreciated that a lot. I read my favorite quote again for the hundredth time and with that resolution in mind I opened my email and started my day.

# 2
## CHAPTER

**11 years ago**

It was a cool summer morning as I watched the sun rise in the east when I got off the bus at my new school. I was a freshman at Memorial High School and it was the very first time I had ever attended a public school. There were so many teenagers surrounding me that all I could hear was loud laughter, talking, yelling, and the sound of the busses hissing as they came to a stop. This is what it felt like to be at a school with more than 50 students and you didn't have all your studies in one classroom. It didn't scare me though. I've been ready for this change for a long time. I followed them inside to the place I would call home for the next 4 years and looked around in amazement. The school was recently renovated so, everything was new, and you could even still smell all the new paint and carpet. I was excited and nervous at the same time. I have always wanted to go to public school because, I wanted to be able to do sports. The private school I attended for eight years had no such programs and it really put a damper on my school experience. I wanted to join a team and now I finally would be able to join one. I had my sights set on the gymnastic team and the dance team. This was a goal I have had for a long time. Don't get me wrong. I loved the private school of attended and I got a great education there. It's just I'm an athlete and I really wanted to join a sports team. That wasn't an option until now. The entrance walls to the school were made of glass and you could see all the way through to the cafeteria. The school colors were crimson and gold and a wide strip of crimson on the top of the walls and ran from the administration office and through rest of the entire school. The school mascot the "Charger horse" was painted proudly a crimson red on the left inner wall of the foyer at the entrance. The floor was covered in thin brown carpet and the walls were painted in yellow. The administration office was on the right as soon as you walked inside and there was a huge space in front of you leading from the front door to the cafeteria. Trophies and pictures covered the walls displaying the great athletic power that the school had. I was proud to be a part of this legacy that was Memorial High school and I was excited to make my mark as well.

The school had 4 major parts and they were all labeled sections A-D. They were all shaped like squares so, it helped to prevent any students from getting lost. To my left and right were two hallways and they led you to section A and Section C of the school building. In between the two hallways on the right was the smaller of the theatre of the two located at the school and directly on the opposite side in between the two hallways on the left was the school library. It didn't really create a hub that the students hung out in however. It seemed that they all preferred to hang out in the hallways. The first section was called section A and it was located directly to the left of the entryway. It housed all the English and Language classes. The school also had a second floor over section A and it was called section B. Both sections had lockers in the hallways and the second floor housed all the math and science classes. Behind the cafeteria was another hallway filled with lockers and this led to Section D. This housed the schools two gymnasiums, pool, weight room, locker rooms, and dance studio. To the right of the cafeteria was what I called the creative section of the school and it fit since it was called section C. It housed the choir rooms, the bigger theatre, home economics, money management, real estate, and child development classes. Thanks to the orientation they had a week ago I knew that the hallway I wanted to take was the first one on my left. My first period class was Freshman English and my locker was conveniently located in the same hallway.

Making my way to my locker was no small feat. There were students everywhere and many were lost looking for their lockers or classrooms. A few even stopped me to ask for directions but, once I told them I couldn't help them, and they would go on to ask another student. I kept walking till I got to the end of the hallway and finally found my locker. The locker was painted in crimson too and in other sections some were even painted in gold. I loved the school colors. It made me feel warm whenever I saw them, and I even liked to look at my school planner that they handed out to us at orientation for that very reason. It was decorated in the school colors and had the current school year listed on the top. That was really cool. I took out the piece of paper with my combination written on it and opened my locker. They were nice and tall and could fit your books, coat, boots, and back pack when winter came. I hung up my jacket, put my books away for my other classes, and walked back to where I came from toward my classroom. Many of the students were talking excitedly as I passed them saying how they were happy to see each other again and how they needed to hang out soon. I saw a couple in the door way of one of the classrooms making out and the students walking inside acted like it was normal as they ducked under them. I didn't see many cliques which was nice, and I hoped that this school didn't really have any but, there was no way I could tell that simply from looking down one hallway.

When I arrived at my classroom I went inside and quickly found a desk exactly in the middle of the room that was vacant. I hated sitting on the sides or in the front of the class and even when I went to see a movie I preferred to sit in the middle. It had a lot to do with my height. Besides, I couldn't stand turning my head for long periods of time for no reason. That hurts your neck so, what's the point of that. If I didn't have to I always sat in the middle. I down sat at my desk and opened my backpack. I took out my book, my binder and my pencil case and began to lay them out neatly on top of my desk. After laying down my book and binder I took out one of the mechanical pencils out of the case. Somehow, I missed the pencil holder at the top of the desk and it rolled on the slippery surface and rolled onto the floor.

"Dang it!" I grumbled as I saw it roll along the floor underneath a desk beside me. Why are the desktops so shiny and slippery anyway! Do they wax these every day! I was about to stand up to retrieve my pencil when I heard a voice next to me.

"Need a little help?" the voice said, and I turned to look at who was speaking to me. When our eyes met I saw a nice looking African-American young man sitting next to me. He had dark skin, small dark brown eyes and full lips like the singer Neyo. I couldn't bring myself to look away.

"When did he get here?" I thought to myself as I continued to stare.

"You'll definitely need this since this is Freshman English. You don't ever want to be without one of them." He said as he handed my pencil back to me. I smiled and thought how nice he was. See, public school isn't as bad as those teen movies made it out to be. I really shouldn't have used those as a point of reference.

"Thank you for your help.... ummm?" I was about to ask him his name when class began, and the teacher started to do roll call. I'd missed my chance. The teacher continued down the list and called my name.

"Sareya Long?"

"Here", I replied but, I made sure to pay close attention when it came to my classmate. I waited patiently as my teacher got around to him. I wanted to know his name.

"Eli Taylor?"

I instantly remembered my mother telling me to never trust a man with two first names. She never told me why. It was just a warning that I always thought was silly. I was about to giggle when the young man who helped responded to the name.

"Present".

"Wow, Eli Taylor huh?" I thought as the teacher wrapped up the roll call. Eli turned to me and smiled, and I saw that he had all perfect teeth. His skin was smooth, his hair was cut low, and he had clean fingernails. He was an attractive young man.

"Alright, let's begin this semester by first announcing the big project you'll have due in two months. It is a group project and you would be responsible for creating a short story. It can be about anything you want it to be if you follow the rubric I'm passing out to you right now. If you stick to it, you should all do a good job. Of course, those who write a great story and follow the rubric to a tee will get the best grades. The groups will consist of two people and I will randomly select your partner right now. Good Luck!" My teacher said as we all sat anxiously waiting to see who we were fated to work with. I immediately broke out in a nervous sweat.

I mean it was our first day, how would we possibly know if we ended up with a good partner or not?

"Oh God, please let me get a good partner. Please let me get a good partner." I silently whispered out loud to myself.

"Team B will be Sareya Long and Eli Taylor."

"What! I just asked for a good partner I didn't ask for the deluxe package!" I thought to myself.

"Your task would be to create a short story at least three pages long. It can be about anything you want but, it must meet the basic English rubric I handed out. Next Team C........"

As my teacher continued down the list of groups I was still stuck on the fact that I was paired with Eli. He looked at me, smiled and I saw once again he had perfect teeth. He was quite handsome but, I didn't like him like that though. I was too busy just trying to make sure I made it on the gymnastic and dance team right now to worry about having a boyfriend. Honestly, I was just glad that he was my partner and maybe, just maybe we could become friends. It looked like we had a promising start.

It was 6pm Monday night two months later and we were at the Elkhart city library finishing up our assignment. I was becoming hungry and I was tired after working on this project for two months.

"My fingers hurt but, I'm finally finished". I said after an hour of typing.

Eli leaned over to look at what we came up with for our final draft. While he stared at it I got goosebumps. Why did he make me feel this way I had no clue? I didn't dislike him close to me but, I kind of liked him close too. After this long of working close together there was no way for me to ignore that fact.

"It looks great. How about I take it home put it in a nice presentation folder and turn it in to class tomorrow?" He asked as I clicked the option to print off the story.

"Thanks Eli. I appreciate it." I was happy that he was finally satisfied with our work. We went through so many revisions I beginning to think we would never finish it.

"I really liked the drama and the comedy you put in the story. I never knew it was possible to do that" he said as he was putting his things away in his backpack.

"Thanks, but I appreciated the points you made about adding more detail. I'm used to talking in detail but, writing it is entirely different." I said as I stood to stretch.

Eli put on his coat and smiled. "I'm just glad we were put on the same team. I'd hate to think what would've happened if we hadn't been put with you."

With that one honest statement I instantly froze. How was I supposed to take that? It was the first time he said anything like this to me before. My heart began to beat a little faster and suddenly, my mind went blank. As if sensing my response, he smiled again.

"I really did enjoy working with you though. It was fun. I hope we get to do it on another project real soon." He picked up his backpack and turned to leave. "I got to get home for dinner Sareya but, I'll see you tomorrow. Have a good night."

As he waved goodbye I somehow managed a breathless goodbye. I was too stunned to say anything. I didn't like him like that so, why was I acting all weird. Darn teenage hormones. I needed to focus. I had gymnastics to try out for next week for the winter season and I had to start getting ready for my dance classes fall performance. Ok, let's be honest it wasn't like I had a line of guys at my door right now. That wouldn't be too bad though. I mean what healthy teenage girl didn't want a guy fawning over her? Was he really fawning?

"AAAAAAAA! This is what my problem is. I analyze things way too much. Ok, Ok, let's just packed up and go home already." I said to myself as I put everything away in my backpack. My dad should've been outside waiting for me anyway and I was too hungry to think straight. I got up from the computer desk and walked into the library foyer. The automatic doors slid open and when I stepped outside I looked up into the evening sky. It was beautiful with colors of red, orange, and gold mixed together. Another day had come to an end and so did our project. I looked out to find my parents car when I saw that they were right in front of me. My father was laughing when I got in the car and I apologized for missing it. I honestly didn't see it. I was too busy looking at the beautiful sunset to look for the car. It wasn't until a cool breeze blew across my nose and I got cold that I remembered he was outside waiting for me.

"How did your study session go?" My father asked while still laughing at me.

"It went great. We finally finished it and I think we're going to get an A." I said proudly.

"That's wonderful Sareya! You two have worked hard so, I'm pretty sure you will get an A. Eli sure seems to be a good partner for you. You should try to keep him close. He seems to bring out the best in you." My father said as he changed the radio station to 106.3.

"Yea".

"I mean if I had someone like that who worked hard and was a good friend I would never let them go. Good friends are hard to come by." He said as he signaled to get back into traffic.

"Yea, you're definitely right about that." I said as I got more comfortable in the back seat. He definitely had a point. I didn't want to ruin something like our friendship and I knew that Eli liked me.

"What am I going to do?" I thought. Slowly, I closed my eyes and listened to the music on the radio as my father pulled off into traffic.

# 3

# CHAPTER

**Present day:**

The clock on the computer showed 5pm and it was time to go home. "Just as I was finishing up too", I thought as I grabbed my purse and coat. I heard a knock at my door and it was Shania.

"Sareya, I know your about to leave but, someone is here to see you." I was about to ask who when the guest walked in the door. It was my best friend LuAnn.

"Hey Girl!" she yelled as she ran towards me. Before I could utter a word, she had me in the tightest hug that only she could give. "I missed you girl, I see your career is going v-e-r-y-well." I blushed a bit and she smacked me on my shoulder. "We have to go to dinner tonight my treat we have two things to celebrate."

"We do! What" I asked. I really didn't care why because we've been close since grade school. We went to church together, went to school together and even got baptized together. In a nutshell I was very happy she was here.

"I just got a job as a software engineer at Artemis!"

I blank my eyes twice. "Are you serious? You're going to be here in Indy with me?" It only took another second for it to sink in and we both started jumping up down from the great news.

"Yea, and I start in a couple weeks so, I need to get my stuff moved down here. They are even helping me to move by paying for my moving expenses, isn't that great!" I hugged her myself this time. We had always spoken of moving to Indy together but, it wasn't possible at the time. Now it was finally happening. "I have so much to do but, I know that you'll help me with it. You've always been good about getting information and taking care of business quickly." She gave me another big hug.

"We have to celebrate this first and I know the perfect place to go for dinner."

An hour later we were seated at an Italian Restaurant with sparkling Moscato in our glasses and goofy grins on our faces. To celebrate this momentous occasion, I took her to our favorite place: Olive Garden. We've loved this restaurant since high school and we always went there to eat before any school dance. It was always the place of choice.

"These breadsticks just keep getting better don't they?" I said realizing how relaxed I was with her. I forgot how nice it felt to be this way. It had simply been too long. "Do you know where you're going to move yet?" She shrugged her shoulders.

"Not yet, I was hoping you'd tell me where the good neighborhoods were then I would see what was available." I nodded my head as I took another bite of my breadstick. LuAnn was never one to argue with getting help. She was never the prideful type. She's always been very indecisive. At 5ft 4 in and weighing 150 she has always been a little overweight. Today dressed in a cute green top and jeans I always thought she was one of the cutest women I had ever met. After hearing her complain over and over about how she wanted to lose the weight I offered to help her but, it never worked out. She could have easily lost it if she ate better and exercised but, she never committed to it or often quit after one day at the gym. I tried to get her to go out with me on numerous occasions to dance but, she wouldn't do that either.

"Alright, sounds good. We can start on that tomorrow." She smiled and did her notorious giggle. "I knew I could count on you. You were never one to procrastinate. Now, I on the other hand tend to wait till the last minute." I looked at her as I took a bite of my salad.

"You know you can't be like that now that you're a Software Engineer at Artemis. They'll drop you faster than a hot potato if you slack off on their products."

"Oh, don't worry about me. My work never suffers. I never procrastinate when it comes to my money." We both laughed and clinked are glasses to that statement.

"We are women hear us roar!"

A couple of hours later it was 9 pm and we were quite full. We had spent the last three hours catching up on each other's lives and now it was time for me to go home. Unlike LuAnn I had work in the morning. The restaurant would be closing in a couple of hours and the music of Italy continued to flow through the speakers. There weren't that many customers in the restaurant now that the dinner rush had come and gone. It was nice being able to hear nothing but the music and the clinking of silverware as the kitchen prepared and cleaned the dishes. My lasagna sat pretty much ravaged and my soup I'd ordered was completely gone. LuAnn had the alfredo and from the look of her plate it was also vacant from her plate. We both groaned and stretched trying to relieve the tightness in our bellies. Right after she stretched she slowly stood up from the table.

"Sareya, I have to go to the bathroom could you wait a minute for me before we leave?" I reached around for my purse and set it on the table.

"Sure, I'll take care of the bill while I'm at it too." She started to protest but, I insisted on treating her as congratulations for landing her new job.

"Thanks, Sareya. You've always looked out for me. I'll have to repay you someday." She smiled and headed off to the bathroom.

I motioned for the waiter to bring me the check and handed her my bank card. While I waited my eyes began to wander around the restaurant following all the glowing orange lights that were lit inside. The looked so calming and beautiful. One could get lost in the lighting ambience itself. As I looked at the ones that were to the right of me I noticed a really nice looking African-American young man sitting at a table right across from me. He was with someone but, I noticed that he kept looking at me. I suddenly started to feel self-conscious. That's just rude! Why would he stare at me while he's out with someone? Our waiter caught my attention at that moment as she brought back my receipt. I broke the eye contact from the young man and thanked the waiter for her good service. I quickly signed the receipt, handed it back to her and turned my attention back to the young man across the room. She thanked me for our patronage and even wished me a good evening but, I was too busy trying to look at the mystery guy again. I wanted to see if he was still looking in my direction. What I saw was the person that he was with him was gone but, he was still there. Not only was he still here but, he was staring directly at me.

He was wearing a red Kangoo hat that matched a three-piece suit black suit with a crimson shirt, silver vest, and solid black pants. He had small brown almond shaped eyes, nice full lips, bald, and smooth brown skin. His hands were big, and his build was definitely on the muscular side. Not too muscular like a body builder but, enough to where if he hugged me he wouldn't accidentally choke me to death. He had on a pair of Stacy Adams polished to the 10th degree and a watch that said he liked fancy things. This man took care of himself.

"You saw him too huh". LuAnn said when she came back to the table and started putting on her coat. Thanks to her the spell was broken and I took a deep breath. I didn't realize I was holding my breath.

"Yea, when did you first notice him? I just saw him while you were in the bathroom."

"Girl, I saw him when he first walked in over an hour ago. He was with someone but, it didn't look personal." Leave it to LuAnn to assess a situation less than 30 seconds. I stood up to grab my purse and coat still uneasy from what just happened.

"I wonder who he is?" I said as I put my coat on.

Just then a huge smile spread across her face. "Wonder no more, he's coming over."

"He is!" I exclaimed frantically as I reached into my purse to grab some gum and my lip gloss. The last thing I wanted was for him to talk to me with chapped lips and garlic breath. I kept facing LuAnn as he made his way over.

"Remain calm, Remain calm. I kept telling myself. "Ah, who am I kidding. I can't be..." Before I knew it the feel of body heat was on my right a very intoxicating men's cologne filled the air as he stood behind me. I somehow managed to gracefully turn to face him and noticed that he was easily 5 ft. 8 in which for me was tall. Standing face to face with him caused me to have to look up to look him in the face. He was the perfect height for me. Up close just made him look even more devastatingly handsome. His skin was so smooth, and he had moisturized full lips and skin. In the winter time that was hard to accomplish sometimes so, I knew that he drank a lot of water. He had broad shoulders and with his button up shirt and vest it made them stand out in the most delicious way. His arms as I noticed before were muscular and looked to have a build like Joe Manganiello from True Blood. I couldn't stop looking at him. This was one man I had to problem looking up to. He extended his hand and smiled at me obviously happy with the response he received.

"Hi, my name is Caius Turel Locke. Everyone calls me Turel." I shook his hand and a feeling of warmth began to envelope my hand. At the same time, I felt an immediate connection to him as if I've always known him. What in the world was this feeling? Dare I say it felt as if my hand belonged in his? It was very daunting.

"My name is Sareya Long, and this is my friend LuAnn Johnson." He let go of my hand and turned to nod toward my friend. When he did the connection was broken.

"Why does everyone call you by your middle name? I asked.

"Oh, my friends thought it sounded more black so, I've been going by Turel since grade school."

"I don't know why they would feel like that about your first name. I like it and find it very exotic. I don't like your middle name. Can I call you by your first name instead of your middle name?"

"I've never been told my name was exotic before." He laughed a small laugh.

"Well, it's a beautiful name and I like it far more than Turel." LuAnn hit me with her elbow then and cleared her throat. I know she was trying to get me to stop but, I really couldn't stand having to call him by that terrible name.

"If you want to call me Caius then I would love to hear my name fall from your lips."

It was then that I saw that his dinner friend was missing. "Weren't you here with someone?"

"I was. It was a business dinner and our meeting was already over. I originally didn't want to come but, I'm glad that I did. If I hadn't I wouldn't have gotten to meet the both of you." He turned back to me, reached into his pocket and pulled out a business card. I watched his hands as he performed the action and noticed how polished and clean his finger nails were. He took care of himself. He smiled as he handed me his card and I saw that he had a great smile. LuAnn elbowed me again and I knew I must have been staring. I made myself look down at his card in my hand and read that he was a Cyber Security Tech at a local tech company.

"You love computers huh?" I said out of nervousness. My friend bumped my arm and I started to blush. He laughed at my comment and I learned that he not only had a beautiful smile but, also a great laugh.

"Actually, I do. I enjoy what I do. I have no complaints. What do you do?" My eyes went down just as LuAnn bumped my arm again. I turned to look at her. How many times do you plan on bumping me!

"Hey, I'm going to go make a phone call and warm up the car. I'll be out there when you're ready to go ok?" She then grabbed her purse, leaned over to me and whispered "Be nice. He seems like a really nice guy. I have a good feeling about him.

"It was nice to meet you Caius. I hope to get to talk to you again soon." She said as she turned to face him again.

"Like wise LuAnn. Have a good night." He said as he shook her hand one last time. With that she winked at me and walked out of the restaurant. Before I knew it, we were alone.

"So, Sareya. What do you do?" He asked.

"What do I do" I repeated the question to myself. "Well, I am the Health Information Manager for Riley's Children Hospital." He put his hands in his pockets and smiled again with his perfect teeth.

"Wow, that's impressive. You must love helping people?" I began to fidget with my purse.

"I do. I also love computers and business. My job encompasses them all." Caius's eyes lit up.

"Is that so? Well, I would love to take you out sometime. A museum perhaps. Do you like art?" I couldn't believe what I'd just heard. Did I just get asked out? "I want to hear what you have to say about the historical art pieces. I've never been to one myself but, I get the feeling that you have a keen eye for it." I couldn't help but smile at that statement. I do love museums. It didn't matter what it was for. I just loved to learn.

"Sure, here's my card." I made sure to write my personal cell number on it and handed it to him.

"Does next Sunday sound good to you? I have something to do this week but, I'll be available by then."

"Yes, that would be great." I replied all the while feeling a nervous sweat forming on my back and underarms. Why was this guy making me feel so flustered? I have never felt this feeling before in my life.

"May I walk you your car?" He asked. Not wanting to end this special meeting I told him yes.

We walked out into the brisk cold January air and it dawned on me that I had a date. Trying to stay calm I managed not to stumble or slip and fall while he was walking me to the car. Thank goodness for my dance training! I took my gloves out of my coat pockets and put them on as the cold air softly blew across my face. Even though it was a mild winter it was still cold at night. No snow on the ground to be seen but, there was water from the rain that had come through the other day. There were other restaurants surrounding this one and one main road that was in between them all. If you wanted to see a movie or go to the mall this was the area of Indy that you wanted to go to. There was plenty of night life and plenty of things to do. There were other spots like this in Indy but, I loved this area so much that my house was only five minutes from here. It was a no brainer when I was looking for a house. Everything I wanted was conveniently located close by.

When we approached my car, I turned to look up into his eyes. I saw on the walk over that LuAnn was on her phone playing Candy Crush so, she wasn't paying us any attention. Caius seeing this took the opportunity to grab my hand again. He must have felt the connection I'd felt earlier too because, once he held it again we both took a quick breath. My heart began to beat faster, and I felt my hands warm up in his grasp. What is this? Dare I say, I even felt safe in his presence? No, that's not possible! It takes time to feel like this towards someone right? How can I feel a connection like this when I've just met the man? Just then he began to rub my hand with his thumb and surprisingly it started to calm me down. Before I knew it, I was very relaxed.

"Is it okay if I call you tomorrow to finalize a time to pick you up?" He asked as he continued to rub my hand with his thumb. This just feels way too good. I don't want him to ever let go of my hand.

"Sure, I work from 8am-5pm so, feel free to contact me anytime."

"Great, I work the same hours so, I'll call you tomorrow then. I look forward to hearing your voice again." he said. I nodded my head and he slowly, reluctantly let go of my hand.

I instantly felt bereft. How come he's the only one who's ever given me this feeling? I've dated a few guys before and I've never felt this before! Why was this man different! I was starting to get frustrated when a brisk January air blew across my face again. It gently helped to calm and ease my mind. Now was not the time to be analytical and plus I knew that I wanted to see him again.

"You have a good night Sareya. I'll talk to you tomorrow." He said as he looked deep into my eyes.

"I look forward to it too Caius. Have a good night."

He turned to walk away, and I watched as he started to walk toward his car. I stopped looking for a second to reach down to open the door when I heard his voice again.

"Have a good night Sareya!" He yelled as we waved to me. Then he turned the corner and was out of sight. His car must have been on the other side of the restaurant.

I smiled, opened my door, and got into the car.

"He seems like fun, doesn't he? Did he ask you out Girl?" LuAnn asked as soon as my butt got into the driver seat.

"Yea, he did." I said obviously still not able to believe it myself.

"AAAAAAAAA! That's what's up! I'm so excited for you girl! When is the date?"

"Sunday." I told her as I pulled out of the parking lot and into traffic.

"Oh, we have to go shopping! You must wear a new outfit! Are you free tomorrow; we can go to the mall and get you a really nice dress..." LuAnn kept going all the way till I dropped her off at her hotel. When I finally acquiesced to going shopping with her on Wednesday after work that finally appeased her. For me, I still was wrestling with the fact that I had a date all the way driving home. How long has it been three years? I get so nervous in his presence will I say something embarrassing. Will I be too honest and turn him off. What have I gotten myself into?

After I got home I proceeded to get ready for bed all the while thinking about Caius. I thought about his smile and the way he laughed. Man, did I love the way he laughed. I thought about the way he spoke and how respectful he was. He was totally different from the men I had dated before. I don't know what made him want to talk to me but I'm glad that he did. I brushed my teeth, put my hair cap on and laid down in my soft bed. The temperature in the house felt good so, I didn't wear any socks in bed tonight either. Slowly, I began to fall into a deep sleep with only Caius on my mind. The last thing I saw was his perfect smile and his hand holding mine.

# 4
# CHAPTER

The sound of my alarm clock going off in my dreams was not a welcome sound the next morning. Well, let's face it. It's not welcome any morning. I am truly not a morning person. The groggy feeling of precious sleep was beckoning me to come back to bed but, my mind wouldn't allow me to do something so tragic apparently. Don't get me wrong I am not a grouchy person nor am I a mean person in the morning. I'm just simply put not awake yet. I am a night owl so, if I had it my way I would prefer to be up till the early morning instead of waking up to it. I looked at the device that has caused me so much pain and anguish and I saw that the bright red numbers read 7:00am. It was time to get up.

I slowly peeled my sheet and blanket off me and turned to put my feet onto the cold wooden floor. This always helped to wake me up in the morning. What better way to wake up than a hit of coldness to run up from your toes to the tip of your head. For me this worked better than any cup of coffee. I made my way into the bathroom, turned the faucet shower all the way to the hot side and sat on my vanity chair to wait for it to warm up. I like my showers pretty hot so, it was nice to have a seat while I waited for it to heat up. After a minute I adjusted the water, made sure it was the perfect temperature and stepped inside. Since my hair style is natural with no perm chemicals in it I don't need to wear a shower cap. This made it so that I could really enjoy the shower for what it truly was. As the warm water rolled across my skin I could feel the warmth and pressure of the rain setting putting ease to my mind. Thanks to that I began to relax, and it started to wander freely and recap what happened last night. I had such a great time hanging out with Luann and eating out at our favorite restaurant. It was great to see her again and learn that she was moving to the same city as me for a job offer. Then I remembered the tailored 3 piece red and black suit, the nicely polished Stacy Adams and then warmth of a man holding my hand for the first time in years.

"Caius!" I yelled in the shower. That's right, I met Caius last night. I took a deep breath as my brain worked hard to pull the memories of last night through my groggy brain. He asked me out, didn't he? It wasn't a dream! We're supposed to be going out this weekend and I'm supposed to go shopping with Luanne and find a dress for it. "AHHHHH!" I yelled in disbelief. If there was anything I hated doing more than anything was shopping for clothes. Why couldn't she just pick it out for me? She knows what I wear right?

"He was real, and I am actually going on a date." I told myself as I started lathering up my loofa. I smiled a goofy grin and got all excited while I cleaned myself and when I finished almost tripped getting out of the shower stall. There was no doubt it. I was truly awake now.

On the way to work I tried to tell myself to remain calm so that I didn't tip off Shania that something big had happened last night. I knew it was probably pointless but, I tried to tell myself this anyway. Once I got off the elevator and walked onto my floor she must have had a beacon on for me because, I didn't even make it two steps before she cornered me in the hallway.

"Good Morning Sareya!" She said in a very sweetish voice.

"Morning Shania." I said as I tried to walk past her.

"Oh no you don't, where do you think you are going?"

"Preferably to the break room to make myself some tea". I said as I tried to move past her again.

"I don't think so. At least not until you tell me why you have this silly look on your face." She said as she leaned in real close as if she was going to inspect me.

"What look? And why do you have to be so close Shania. Man, back up."

"Nope? Why don't tell me before I started asking a million questions? You know I will." She was right about that. Shania was like a pitbull. Once she grabbed a hold of something she never let it go.

"Fine, just let me get my tea first and meet me in my office."

"AAAAAA, something did happen? I knew it! I knew it as soon as I saw you stepped off the elevator with that goofy grin on your face." My eyes grew huge hearing that she could tell first thing this morning. I guess that self-pep talk didn't help at all.

"Girl, calm down and get in my office. I'll be there in a second." I said as I lightly pushed her shoulder, so she would move out of the way.

"Ok." She said as she skipped down to my office door. Is this girl really skipping? I shook my head and sighed thinking about how this was going to go. While I made my tea I even contemplated lying to her. I knew that she would take this and make it bigger than it was. It wasn't like I thought she'd jinx it or anything. It was more like I didn't want to believe in something when it hadn't even happened yet. I made my way into my office and mentally prepared myself for the interrogation that was about to occur.

It was about 10 minutes later when I had I told her about everything that happened up to right before he asked me on a date when she began to bombard me with questions.

"So, you and Luann went out to eat and you saw a guy sitting across the room from you? Shania asked.

"Yes." I answered.

"When you go up to leave he came over to the table?

I nodded my head.

"You really didn't notice him until the end of your dinner"

"Yep." I answered curtly.

"Wow, I would have thought you would've noticed him before that. After you introduced yourselves he shook your hand, right?"

I nodded my head and began to blush.

"Wait, are you beginning to blush. I have never seen you do this before Sareya. Why are you blushing? Did he kiss you or something?" She asked with extreme excitement as if we were teenagers again.

"Oh, my goodness. No, Shania. He didn't!" I mumbled as I lowered my head on my desk from embarrassment.

"Then why are you acting so weird if he didn't try to kiss you? What else could make you feel like this?" She asked with now a look of confusion on her face.

"He held my hand." I mumbled.

"He did what"

I raised my head and repeated what I said. "He held my hand." She looked at me and turned her head to the side like a dog when they don't understand what we are saying. Then again, I didn't understand it either so, who was I to judge her reaction.

"He held my hand" I repeated.

"He..held..your..hand?" She said slowly as if seriously considering what I had just told her.

I took a deep sigh. "Yes, and the way my hand warmed up to his touch was frightening. I've never had that happen before.

"Really?" She said with a look of shock on her face.

"Mmhmm, I also felt a feeling of belonging as if I was always supposed to be with him." I continued. I know this all sounds weird but, it's how I felt just from him holding my hand. When we parted, and he had to let go I was sad and he looked sad too. I think he felt the same thing I did."

"Wow! That sounds powerful." She said with a now a look of wonderment on her face. Who know she could make so many faces.

"It was so scary Shania. I don't know how to handle these emotions. A part of me wants to talk to him right now for example but, another part is saying it would be doing too much after just meeting him last night." Finally, Shania seemed to understand the seriousness of my situation and calmed her happy tail down.

"Hey! Why don't you call him during lunch?"

"I don't know if I should Shania. He did say he would call me today. I figured I'd get a call after work though. I don't want to bother him on his lunch break. Besides, I don't even know when it is."

"Fine. If he doesn't call you by 8pm then you call him ok!" Shania said with a stern look in her eye. I felt like I was being threatened by the dating police.

"Ok, just calm down. I know you're as excited as I am but, you shouldn't start barking threats at me when I just met the man. Let's see if he calls and if he doesn't then I will call him tomorrow. How does that sound to you?" I asked with a complacent look on my face hoping that she would finally drop the subject.

"Alright. You better call him too." She acquiesced.

"I will. Now leave my office." I said with a sigh and stood to push her out my door.

As soon as she was out of my office I closed the door shut and leaned my back against the cold door. Even though I agreed with Shania about calling him it didn't mean I wanted to do it. Shoot, it was difficult enough just getting through a normal conversation with man let alone while he was holding my hand. I walked back to my desk and plopped down into my leather chair. How am I supposed to do this without looking like I'm desperate? Come to think of it, is there a way to do this without looking desperate? I shook my head and took another deep breath. Slowly, I calmed down and looked at my computer screen. It was still turned off. In all the fuss this morning I forgot to turn the darn thing on. What is wrong with me? My keyboard colored in black was laying in front of me and almost looked like it was trying to say stop thinking about a man and get to work. With that I turned on my computer and started my day.

"Sareya! It's lunch time." Shania yelled as she peeked her head in my door.

"Really? Good, because I am starving." I said as I grabbed my purse and my light jacket. The beauty of not having any meetings this week was that we got to have lunch on time for once. We all decided to eat out every day and celebrate not having to have our lunches cut short or rushed due to meetings.

"I feel like I'm on vacation, don't you?" She asked after she pushed the button for the elevator.

"I do. Where are we going today?" I asked while I buttoned up my jacket.

"Hmmmm. How about that new Mongolian BBQ place a couple of blocks from here? I heard it has really good food and really great prices." You could always count on Shania to ball on a budget.

"Sounds good to me." I said as the elevator doors opened. "Let's go."

Shania and I walked to the restaurant and were happy to see that we didn't have to wait too long to get a booth. It was placed between an Italian and a Chinese restaurant it seemed like a good spot to put a Mongolian Restaurant to me. Inside it had medium brown wood floors and the walls were decorated in various shades of red and yellow textured wallpaper. They offered booths and tables but, if you sat at a booth it came with hooks to hang your purse and coat. It had good lighting coming in from the windows and it gave off a fun atmosphere. It was my kind of place to eat. Our waiter came quickly and we both ordered Coca-Cola for our beverages. Before the waiter walked away she handed us our menus and pointed out on the table top sat the menu specials and the desserts menu.

I browsed through mine for a while and Shania skimmed through hers. Everything looked so good. It was hard to choose. We both finally decided on the chicken fried rice sweet & sour burrito and when our waiter came back with our drinks we were ready to place our order. After our menus were taken I checked my phone. I knew I shouldn't have any messages or missed calls from work but, I wanted to see if Caius had tried to get in contact with me. When I looked at my screen it showed no new messages or missed calls.

"He hasn't called yet huh?" Shania said while was I putting my phone away.

"What makes you think that was what I was checking my phone for? Why couldn't I have been checking it for work or getting on a form of social media?" Shania smirked at me.

"Well let's see first: Our boss isn't here so nobody would be calling or texting you. And two: You don't even get on social media's like that and since when did you ever call them social media's?" Ok, she had me there. I'm barely on Twitter as it is and the only time I'm on Facebook was to check in on my relatives to see how they were doing. This girl knows me too well.

"Yea, I was checking to see if Caius called or texted me. I don't know why I did though. I already figured he wouldn't get in contact with me till he got out of work anyway. He said he has the same work hours that I have."

"Hmm. Ok. Well, tell me did he ask you out on a date?" She asked with her eyes all wide. I thought I'd told her this already but, apparently, I hadn't. We must have gotten stuck at the part with him holding my hand.

"Yea, he wants to go out on Sunday."

"OOOOOOOOO" She squealed.

"You're so silly Shania." I said as I shook my head. "Seriously, he did ask me out this Sunday. My best friend Luann whom you saw yesterday is going to take me out shopping for a dress to wear for the date."

"Oh, can I come too" She asked with a look of pleading in her eyes. My goodness between Shania and Luann what are they trying to do subjugate me?

"Please! She said again while I thought it over.

"Fine, you can come" I regrettably agreed. I know I haven't had a man in a long time and I know I hate shopping but, come on!

"Y…." I cut her off before she could continue.

"But, only if you behave yourself. Do you understand?" I implored her.

"Yes, I get it. I promise to be on my best behavior."

"Thank you." I said as I got up to pick out my food and watch it cook on the grill.

Lunch was great, and I had plenty left over for dinner tonight which was always a good thing. The rest of my day went smoothly, and Shania started to already be on her best behavior. I didn't even think that was feasible but, here she was being cooperative. I guess she wanted to show me that she was able to comply with my requests after all the questioning she put me through. However, as I was driving home I became irritated again. Why is my personal life so exciting to these two anyway? It's not like anything exciting even happened yet. For crying out loud, I just met the man. At this rate I won't even make it to the date because, these two women will make me lose it way before that even happens. I didn't think Luann would even agree with having someone she didn't even know join us to go shopping but, her reply text said, "The more the merrier." Seriously! It was official. These two are really going to wear me out.

It was sprinkling a bit when I got to my subdivision and drove into my garage. The temperature today was 40 degrees so; it still wasn't cold enough to snow. I was very happy to have clear roads to drive on this winter and I knew with it being January that could always change. I opened my door and hung up my jacket on one of the hooks I put on the wall. It was very nice to have especially when there was snow or mud on my shoes. I could easily leave them at the back door and not have to worry about them tracking them through the house. I placed my leftovers on the counter and went into my bedroom. I began to take change my clothes when I decided to take a shower. It wasn't like I was sweaty but, I just felt like being extra clean. After the shower I changed into my pajamas into my favorite comfortable pajamas which were the same pair I liked to have when I watched my favorite shows on TV. I had a pair of thin blue cotton pajamas that I loved that I wore most of the time. The shirt had long sleeves and the bottoms were full length pants. I had another pair like these that were also very comfortable but, they were thicker and were made for colder weather. My house contained heat very well so, I didn't have to use the heat like that on a regular basis. I could wear thin cotton pajamas and I will feel nice and warm with my thermostat set on 72 degrees. Having Eco-friendly products in your home was a smart purchase.

I walked back into the kitchen and looked at the clock on the microwave. It read 7:55. "It's almost time for "New Girl to come on!" I thought as I hurried to set the timer for my food. While I waited the minute necessary to cook my food I turned on the TV and turned it to the FOX channel so that I didn't miss a single second of the show. I absolutely loved "New Girl" and I found it without a doubt hilarious. I never missed an episode. I preferred to watch it live but, when that wasn't possible I would set it to record on my DVR. Tonight, would be a live viewing. A few seconds later I heard the microwave bell go off and I looked at the clock to see that I had only 3 minutes before the show came on. I quickly poured myself a cup of Cranberry Apple juice and had a seat on my comfortable couch. I set my cup on the end table with a coaster underneath and prepared myself for the comedy magic that was about to unfold.

-Ring! Ring! - I heard my phone yell from the kitchen counter.

"Why isn't my phone over here with me?" I thought as I stood to go get my phone. I went to answer it annoyed by the fact that I had just gotten comfortable and my show was about to start. I was going to immediately ignore the call but, on the screen in big letters on my I-phone was the name Caius. I forgot that I had put his name in my phone after lunch to make sure I knew it was him and wouldn't ignore his call.

"He is really calling me." I thought as my hands suddenly grew prickly and sweaty. I stared at the screen not moving at all. It was as if I thought it would stop ringing if I wished it to. It didn't stop ringing. The worst part was I have my phone to ring at least 6 times so, that it gave me enough time to answer it due to work and such. What was only a few seconds felt like hours as I decided on what to do about answering the call in my hand. This small contraption was the only things standing between me and my near future. This was the only thing standing between me and possibly finally finding true happiness. Didn't I deserve that? If I believed that why wouldn't I answer the phone? With that last thought I made up my mind to take the next step. I was worth it. My finger began to move and on the last ring I slowly touched the green accept button to answer the call. There was no turning back now.

35

# 5

# CHAPTER

"Hello" I spoke meekly into the cellphone.

"Hi Sareya. How are you this evening?" Caius asked in a warm low tone. His voice wasn't deep, but it wasn't high either. It was perfectly in the middle. I made my way back to the couch and sat back down into my favorite spot. The comfortability that it once had was now gone though. There was no way I would be able to get comfortable with him on the other end of this phone.

"I'm doing well. How about yourself?" I said proudly. I couldn't believe my voice wasn't shaking.

"I'm also doing well. Did you have a good day today at work?" He asked.

"I did." Memories of the conversation and the lunch I had with Shania filled my mind again. How do I tell him that I was thinking about him pretty much for the entire day? "I thought about you all day today." I said before I even realized I'd said it. In a way I was glad I did. I'm not the shy type and I wanted him to know that I was thinking of him. Is that really so wrong?

"I thought about you to Sareya." He replied. I guess it wasn't a bad idea to tell him. Then I heard him give a warm chuckle. "The truth of the matter is I haven't been able to get you out of my mind since the moment I met you. Today was a very busy day and I couldn't wait till I got home to call you so, I could hear your voice again.

"You like my voice?" I asked even though I knew it was a very stupid question to ask. Why did I have to ask another forward question? I just met the man!

"Oh, yes. It's very soothing to me." He said. Really? Never mind then. At this rate speaking my mind is really working out for me. I'm not changing a thing.

"I missed hearing yours too. Tell me what type of things did you have to do at work today? Did you have to take another potential client out the dinner?"

No! Thank goodness." He said laughing as if he wouldn't be able to stomach having to do that again. "Although, I don't regret for a second taking the one out last night because, if I hadn't I would've never met you."

"Well…. I said blushing profusely. I can honestly say I'm glad you did too."

"To answer your question though, I had meetings today about a new security program that my office will be promoting soon and we have to attend meetings for the next couple of weeks to learn the ends and outs of the new software program. I'm one of the main people who will be implementing and possibly selling it so, I have to attend." He laughed.

"It sounds pretty boring"

"Ah no. It's just like being in college all over again. Tons of paperwork to read through, simulations to go over, and of course the long lectures you had to sit through. All for sake of knowledge. I don't the selling part but, I love the implementing part."

"That's good. I'm glad to hear that you're enjoying yourself."

"Yea, thanks. Well, how about you? How was your day at work?" I took a deep breath and stepped out on faith that I wouldn't sound stupid in my response. The last thing I wanted to do was sound like an idiot.

"It was good. Unlike you my boss is out of the office for a week so, we don't have any meetings scheduled which is great. My department feels like we're on vacation." I laughed into the phone.

"It sounds like your department gets along very well."

"Oh yea! We have birthday parties, Carry-ins every chance we can get, and we're always goofing around. What I love about my department is that we're more like family than co-workers."

"Wow! That must be nice?" He said.

"It is. I wouldn't trade it for the world." I smiled into the phone.

"I can hear you smiling." He said.

"You can?"

"Yep, I wish I could see it. You have a beautiful smile."

"Thank you." I said as I began to blush even more. Who know that was even possible? I must have been quiet for a bit because he asked me if I was okay.

"Hmm? Oh, yes, I 'm fine. You just made a bit nervous is all."

"Ah, I didn't mean to do that Sareya. The last thing I want to do is make you uncomfortable." He said with an underling confident tone. "Although, I find it very refreshing that you speak so openly with me. That's something you find very often. It makes me want to be more open with you too."

"It does?" I said shocked. My skin was prickly at this point and I had begun to have a nervous sweat from head to toe. "Before I have my date I have to get this under control." I told myself as I repeatedly pulled my shirt from my chest in an effort cool myself down.

"Mmhmm. I want you to know what I'm thinking and how I feel too. Does it bother if I do that?" He asked.

"No, I find it refreshing too. Even though it makes me nervous." We both laughed at my statement and I finally decided to go change my clothes into a tank top and some shorts. This was just not going to work. "So, what time did you get off work today?" I asked him right before I put him on speaker phone and walked to my bedroom.

"5pm. Even though it felt like it was later than that. You can only sit through so much lecture in an uncomfortable sit till you feel like you have to make a run for it you know?" He laughed.

"That's very true. I said as I walked into my closet and pulled out the drawer with my tanks and shorts in them. "How many breaks to you guys get?" I asked as I switched my clothes from my thin pajamas to a yellow tank top and a pair of black cotton shorts that I liked to wear for my Jazz and Ballet dance classes. Yes, this feels so much better.

"We get four 15-minute breaks not including an hour lunch but, they are not nearly long enough." He groaned.

"I'm sorry. Maybe there is something that can make this go by a lot faster for you." I giggled as I made my way back to the living room.

"Actually, I get the feeling that you would be a huge part of helping me get through this." He said.

"Oh? How is that?" I said as I sat back down on the couch. I knew I wouldn't be able to get comfortable right now but, at least I'd be able to breath and not sweat to death.

"Well, our date in a couple of days is one way you're helping me."

"…a…a" I had nothing to say.

"I was thinking I would take you to the Indianapolis Museum of Art. I hear they have many great exhibitions but, one I'm really interested in is the one about the Contemporary artwork of Japanese Ceramics. Is that something you would be interested in seeing with me?" He said with a hopeful tone.

"I'd love to!" I said a bit too enthusiastically. "I love Japanese culture and have always wanted to go there to visit and learn more about their heritage. I would love to go with you." I said while my heart felt like it was bursting out of my chest. I had never met another man who loved art and Japanese art at that. Can this get any better?

"Great! I am very happy to hear that you love the idea. The museum opens at 12pm so, do you mind if I pick you up?"

"Sure, I live about 20 minutes from there so, 11:30 will be perfect."

"Alright. 11:30am it is. I can't wait."

The next day I was practically glowing. I slept very well, and I found myself for the first time in who knows how long that I was looking forward to the shopping trip my friends and are were going to make in a couple minutes. It was currently 4:45pm and I knew any second my Shania was going to come running into my office. Luann said she'd meet us at the mall so, Shania wanted to ride with me. She takes the bus to work since she lives closer and plus it helps her save on her gas tank. I didn't mind. I enjoyed her company and honestly didn't feel like driving today. I figured I'd leave that to her to do while I relaxed my brain from the 8 hours of eye straining I did looking at the computer all day. Just as 4:55pm popped up on my screen Shania came walking briskly through my door.

"Sareya? Are you ready to go?" I guess she would ask that question. I was still sitting at my desk but, I was daydream about what I wanted to wear for my date.

"Yes, sorry. I'm ready to go." I quickly grabbed my purse along with my light coat and together we made our way to the elevator.

"Alright, hand me your keys."

"Why? We're not even down there yet?" I asked

"In case you change your mind and try to make a break for it." She said as she extended her flat palm to me. She had a very serious look in her eye. I knew I wouldn't run but, I understood why she would be concerned. I took my keys out of my purse and set them in the middle of her small hand.

"Feel better now" I asked with my right eyebrow raised.

"Yea." She said at the same time as the elevator dinged and the doors opened.

The drive over was smooth and Shania as always, a good defensive driver. I was already knowledgeable about this from the times we would hang out so, it was a no brainer to let her drive my car. Even though she told me she only offered to drive to make sure I didn't make a break for it I still didn't mind her doing the driving. We decided to go to Greenwood Park mall and it was only about 15 minutes south of the hospital. Somehow, the traffic wasn't bad getting their even though it was after 5pm in the early evening. The parking lot wasn't too busy, and we were able to park right close the mall doors. That was one of the things I hated about going to the mall during the busy seasons. I was still wearing my shoes from work which were a pair of 2 in heel boots so, they weren't exactly made for doing a lot of walking in. If I had thought it through better I would've worn some flats but, it was too late now. I did love the design of the mall and how they decorated the outside. The exterior was done in all stone ranging in sizes and shades of brown/greys. It had a stores and restaurants lining the sides of the mall so, you could easily see where a store was in case you intended to only go one specifically and park directly in front of it. At the front of the mall sat a water fountain and a wide courtyard for you to walk to the main doors. With the stone design proudly on display it gave the feeling of sturdiness as you pulled up and made you feel that these stores weren't going anywhere.

When we arrived the temperature outside was 36 degrees and a slight wind was blowing as we made our way to the sliding main entrance doors. The smell of the restaurants inside were in the air and I quickly became hungry. I hadn't eaten since lunch and besides, my eyes were set on Chick-Fil-A for dinner. It never failed. Every trip I would make to the mall I would crave Chick-Fil-A when it was time to go. If I didn't get it there would be a huge issue and you didn't want to be the one to prevent me from getting my treat. When we stepped into the doors I saw Luann waiting on the inside for us and she was waving her arm very excitedly.

"Hey Girl! You ready to pick out an outfit that he's going to love?" She asked as we approached her. I nodded my head and put my hands in the pockets of my jacket.

"I assume you've already planned out this shopping trip, haven't you?" I asked fully knowing that she had.

"Of course! We have to make sure that you look your best, don't we?" She said as she turned to say to hi to Shania.

After the introductions were complete Luann announced her battle plan and we were on our way. I was excited to say the least but, I was uncomfortable with the amount of time it would take to do this. Shania and Luann were great at dressing themselves so, I knew I was in good hands. It was more like wondering what they would think I would look pretty in since; I didn't pay attention to fashion that much. I decided to just sit back and enjoy the ride.

"OOOO Girl! Let's go in here. They have some cute dresses that I think you'd love and you could wear on a date." Luann said after seeing the sign for "Amore" a new clothing store in the mall. They had good prices and good quality clothes from what I had heard.

"Ok, let's go." I said as I turned to go into the store.

Shania and Luann looked at each other in shock at the fact that I was being so agreeable about all of this. They didn't say anything to me though. I guess they were treating me like a scared cat and decided to just proceed inside the store along with me. That was a smart idea. Besides I could take flight any second, right? Once inside I saw an assortment of long and short dresses that came in colors ranging from gold to black. I walked along the grey granite that covered the floor of the store and heard my heels clicking as I walked. It was a comforting sound and disturbing at the same time. It made me think of my mother when she used to wear them to special occasions as well as church. It also reinforced the fact that I was a woman and that I was now fully an adult. I was halfway in to the store when I came across a mannequin that was wearing a navy-blue skater dress with a v cut in the front that was covered in a black see through lace. The arms were sleeveless which was great for me since I sweat when I was nervous, and it also had a black trim that came wrapped around the entire bottom part of the skirt. The cut wasn't too low, and the skirt went to the top of the mannequin's thighs. It was beautiful!

"I like this…." I said in a whisper and in awe. Suddenly I felt both behind me as if they'd been there all along.

"You do!?" They both replied in unison.

"Yes, I think it resembles me perfectly. Fun, athletic, and ladylike. Don't you" I said as I turned to face them both while still holding onto the fabric.

"You must like it if you won't even let go of it." Luann said with her right eyebrow raised. I felt like a kid in a candy store that wouldn't let go of the candy bar they wanted.

"Let me get your size then!" Shania said with a squeal!

I walked my way to the dressing room and waited for her to hand me the dress to try on. I hoped it fit. I really liked it. A couple of seconds later I heard a knock at the door.

"Here you go Sareya." Shania said as I opened the door.

"Thanks." I said and closed the door.

Removing my clothes only took a minute because, I was too excited to put the dress on. I pulled it over my head and gently pulled it down to cover my bodice. It felt good and it felt really soft. I wonder what type of material this was. I was confident that it fit so, I walked out to show my friends the dress without even looking into the mirror. The reactions were not expected at all.

"I love it, I love it, I love it! Luann yelled as she jumped up and down. She was always easy to read but, even I was surprised by her reaction.

Shania nodded her head and walked around to inspect every nook and cranny of the dress to make sure nothing was too tight or too loose. When she finished was standing in front of me again and a huge smile came across her face.

"It's perfect Sareya! You picked out a beautiful dress. With your short torso and long legs, you look absolutely stunning." She explained.

"How do you feel about the dress now that's it's on? Do you like on you to you? Does it feel good?" Luanne asked.

"It feels wonderful on me but, I don't know how it looks yet?"

"You haven't looked in the mirror?" They yelled in unison.

"Sorry, no. I was too excited to see what you both thought."

"What matters the most is what you think and how you feel Sareya?" Shania said.

"Here look into the mirror" Luann said as she put her hands on my shoulders and turned me to face the mirror on the wall behind me.

What I saw took my breath away. There before me stood a stunning young woman with long strong legs and high cheekbones that glowed in contrast to the navy blue with her caramel colored skin. I loved who I saw in the mirror.

"I love it too. I'm getting it." I declared as I made my way back into the dressing room to change.

"Alright! We'll be out here waiting for you." Shania yelled.

With the purchase of my date dress in hand I gladly made my way with my friends to pick out a pair of shoes to go with it. I didn't see any that stood out to me so, Shania and Luann had a field day rummaging through the two shoe stores we went to find a pair that went perfectly. They succeeded in finding a pair of grey closed toe boots and as icing on the cake a pair of silver earrings for me to wear with them as well. The earrings had a navy-blue ball in the center of four thin dangles that hung off the bottom. They were exquisite.

"Thank you so much guys. I really do appreciate it. I know I was apprehensive at first about this whole shopping trip but, I've had a great time and I've learned so much more about myself. I couldn't thank you enough. We have to do this again." I said after we'd gotten our food and were sitting down at one of the food court tables.

"Anytime. I mean it" Shania said.

"Me too. Count me in. I had a great time as well." Luann said with a mouthful of fries in her mouth.

I laughed as I took a bite of my nugget from Chick-Fil-A with some Chick-Fil-A sauce on it. It was sublime.

# 6
## CHAPTER

After I dropped off Shania, I drove home, took a shower and had just gotten my pajamas on when I heard the ringtone for Caius begin to play on my phone. I lifted the phone off the bed and slid over the bar to answer the call. This time I wasn't as nervous.

"Good evening"

"Good evening. How are you" He asked me in his warm voice. Oh, how I missed his voice. It felt like I could be enveloped in peace just from simply the sound of his voice alone.

"I'm doing well. How are you?"

"I'm good. Did you have a good day? He asked.

"I did. I got to hang out with my friends today. It's been a long time since I'd done anything like that so, I feel very refreshed today."

"I'm glad to hear that Sareya."

My heart instantly stopped. I'm not used to him saying my name. There went the composure I just had. I broke out in a nervous sweat again and quickly changed out my pajamas.

"How was your day today? I know you are currently in workshops till Saturday learning that new program. Is that going very well, or have you almost lost it yet?" I laughed while I changed into a pair of short and a tank top.

"Nope, not yet. You'd be proud of me. Even an adult has a hard time sitting for long periods of time sometimes. I find the breaks to be too short but, I make due. It helps that my co-worker is hilarious and likes to crack jokes all the time."

"That's nice. I know that many of them probably go on smoke breaks, too don't they? I don't smoke so; I would feel lonely at first when we would have things like that too. I'd be the only one still by the meeting room waiting for it to start."

"I know what you mean. I don't smoke either so, I got used to going outside and playing on my phone away from the smokers. Candy Crush became my new favorite game. At least until my co-worker started hanging out with me during our breaks." He laughed.

"I never got into games like that myself." I giggled. "I'm more into time management games like Diner Dash and Wedding Dash. Those games get my blood pumping every time."

"I've heard of those but, I haven't tried them myself. I'll have to give them a try."

"You should. I found that they help by keep me organized and my thought process fast. The ability to multi-task is a very powerful thing." I said proudly.

"I think I can do that?"

"Really? I heard men didn't have the ability to multi-task like women can." I said.

"I've heard that too but, I don't believe it. I also think that I could get a better score at the game than you can." He said with boldness.

"Do you now? I would love to see you try" I said.

"Well, well, well. You sure sound very confident? He said. I'm pretty sure he was grinning on the other end.

"We will see, won't we? In the meantime, I highly suggest you practice because we will have a showdown. I never back down from a challenge."

"Trust me I will. On another subject are you excited about our date?"

"Of course." I replied. I walked into my walk-in closet and looked at the dress hanging up waiting to be worn in a couple of days. "I've even been preparing for it."

"I'm glad to hear you have. The days can't go fast enough in my opinion."

"Me either." I said before I realized what I'd said. I covered my mouth with a slap and began to blush.

"I heard that Sareya. Don't be scared of what you just admitted to me. I'm happy you feel that comfortable with me. The truth is I can't get enough of your honesty. I feel like I can ask you anything and you will tell me the truth. It is so invigorating to not have to play games with someone for once. I don't have to wonder how you feel about me because, you always tell me. I can't get enough of that so, please don't stop."

With those words…. Caius words I began to calm down. I walked back into my room, removed my hand from my mouth and laid down on my bed. He makes me feel so good about myself it's almost surreal. He doesn't even know me yet but, he can already see the good in me.

"Thank you, Caius. I feel the same way. I too was used to not knowing where I stood in relationships and it drove me nuts trying to figure it out. That's probably why I'm so honest with you now."

"No, I think that's just who you truly are. I can tell" He said with certainty. I couldn't help but smile at that statement. It almost made me want to cry tears of joy. For the first time in my life I have found someone who can see me. The real me. I couldn't wait for our date on Sunday.

The rest of the week was so good I couldn't believe it. The weather stayed in the 40's, there was no snow in the forecast till a couple of days after my date, and I talked to Caius every day after work. He always called at 8pm and instead of watching TV I would talk to him. I couldn't think of a better way to spend my evenings. At work Shania offered to help me get ready for my date so, here I was sitting in my bathroom while Shania and Luann got me ready for my date. Luann showed up out of blue and I didn't think that she would be able to help. When she arrived at 10am I was too thrilled. Shortly after her came Shania and they busily got me ready for my date in a couple of hours.

"You said he'll be here at 12, right?" Luann asked as she painted my finger nails. She had bought a nice silver and clear nail polish to accent my outfit. It was very pretty, and it also had a little glitter in it.

"Yep."

"Alright then we will make sure we have you ready in time. There's nothing worse than not being ready when your date comes to pick you up right?" Shania said. She offered to do my hair for me after seeing a picture and demonstration on YouTube. She decided to give me a Fro-hawk.

"Your right about that." Said Luann as she moved to start painting the nails on my other hand.

"Thank you guys so much. I can't thank you enough for this." I looked into the mirror in front of me and watched as the ladies worked their magic.

"By the way, where you two going for your date? A movie?" Shania asked.

"We're going to an art museum." I said proudly.

"Wow? I have never gone on a date to an art museum before. This guy must be really cultured. I pray I meet a guy like that too" Luann replied.

"I must say that is different. He gets points for that for sure." Shania said.

"I thought it was odd at first too but, I love museums. The fact that he asked to take me to one for our first date spoke volumes to me. I couldn't help but, get excited about it." I explained.

"I agree with you. I think dates should be more focused on interaction. If you go to the movies, you can't talk and get to know each other. However, when you go somewhere that encourages you to talk to the other person like putt putt, bowling, or museums that makes the conversation naturally happen." Shania stated.

"Your right about that Shania. I wished a man would take me out to places that encourage us to talk to each other. I think many men think the movies is the best option for both parties involved. They don't have to talk, and they get to hold your hand or try to kiss you." Explained Luann.

"I hate that too." I yelled. I looked into the mirror and saw that I had accidentally startled the girls. They stopped to look at me for a second checking to see if I was getting upset. "Sorry, I was just saying that I too get annoyed when a man asks to take me on a date to the movies. We can't get to know each other when we can't talk to each other and I'm sorry I'm annoyed when you try to talk to me during the movie. It's inappropriate and I didn't pay my hard-earned money to miss a second of a movie that I'm going to see. No scratch that, I don't care if it's his money or mine. If I went to see it, I'm watching it." I said. My friends and I laughed so hard that Luann almost dropped the nail polish on the floor.

At 11:30 am my friends were finished, and I was ready to go on my first date in over 2 years. They had done my makeup in a natural way by using only earth tones for my eyeshadow and a dark plum lip gloss for my lips. They wanted the entire outfit to balance out and plus they knew I didn't wear makeup like that. I preferred to be natural. I stood to look at myself in the mirror and I was very pleased with the results.

"You guys did a very good job. If I had the money, I'd hire you two as my stylist and makeup team." I joked.

"You couldn't afford us. But thanks anyway." Luann said as she laughed and stuck her tongue out at me.

Luann and I walked out into the living room and sat down to eat my lunch with Shania. She had ordered us some Chinese food and had taken the liberty of laying out the plates and silverware for us, so we could sit down and enjoy our meal.

"I love Orange chicken and fried rice." I said after swallowing bite of food.

"That's all you ever eat. Don't you like the noodles" Luann asked

"Nope, I only like certain meats and fried rice. I know I'm weird." I said. She shook her head at me. Obviously, I've disappointed her.

"Well, I enjoy all forms of Chinese food. I'm not picky like you are." Shania said.

"I'm sorry I'm so weird." I said.

"It's ok. We still love ya." Luann said.

"By the way, are you guys going anywhere after the museum?" Shania asked.

"I don't know. He didn't mention going anywhere else." I said.

"He might you never know. I know I'm always hungry from walking around for a couple of hours." Luann said.

"Very true. If you need a recommendation on where to eat there is a steakhouse a couple miles from there that I heard is really good. I'll text you the address." Shania said.

"Thanks Shania." I said

No, problem. I know you prefer a fun atmosphere along with good food so, I figured this will be right up your alley." Shania replied.

Twenty minutes later the girls were all packed up and ready to go. I hugged them both and thanked them again as they walked out the door. I'm truly blessed to have friends like them I thought as I closed the door. I promised them that I would text them as soon as I got home to let them know I was ok and I would talk to them tomorrow about the date. They were as excited as I was demanding to know every detail of what transpires today. I laughed to myself as I thought about Shania's face when she realized what time it was. They didn't want to be here when Caius arrived, and they rushed to grab their things and hurry out the door. I guess that was a good thing. I know Luann didn't want to leave since she hadn't met him yet but, she reluctantly left when Shania asked her to give her a ride.

It was now 11:55 and Caius was going to be pulling up any second to pick me up for our first date. Our…first…date…. Wow, I couldn't wait for him to get here and it was then I realized I didn't know what car he'd be driving. I laughed to myself and thought good thing I noticed that, or I would've been nervous when a strange car pulled into my driveway. I went into the living room and sat on the love seat which faced the window looking out into the front yard. The TV was to my left and it was turned off. I wanted to be ready when I saw him pull up to my house.

A couple of minutes later I saw an SUV slowly pass my front yard and then turn into my driveway. A second later the car was turned off and the front door was opened. Out stepped Caius. He was right on time. He was dressed in a pair of blue jeans folded at the foot that fit his frame and a v neck brown sweater with a white shirt underneath. The sweater matched the brown that was in the blue jeans and he wore a pair of white and brown striped Adidas to bring it all together. On his head he wore an old school grey Kangoo hat that was long in the front and hugged his head in the back. I liked those hats and I especially liked them on bald headed men. One thing was for sure, this man really knew how to dress himself.

He didn't look nervous at all as he approached my front door. In fact, he looked happy. He went out of view as he stepped onto my front step to ring the doorbell. I rose off the couch making sure I was very careful not to run and make myself sweat. The last thing I wanted to do was sweat despite having a sleeveless dress on. I opened the door and smiled as I Caius appeared before me in full view again. Man, it felt like it's been forever since I've last seen him.

Caius's eyes grew huge as he looked at me from head to toe. This being the first time he's seen me in a dress; I was hoping that this would be the reaction I was going to get from him. He smiled his perfect smile and chuckled to himself.

Instantly the smell of his cologne filled my nose again and I remembered the night we met in full detail. "I have to ask him what he's wearing one day." I thought to myself. He opened his mouth a few times but now words would come out.

"…a…y…." He was speechless. My confidence skyrocketed to the top of the charts. He rubbed the back of his neck, looked me up and down again, and shook his head with a smile.

"Caius, are you okay?" I asked reveling in his reaction.

"Forgive me Sareya. He took a moment to take a breath to compose himself. "You are altogether beautiful, my darling; there is no flaw in you." He said in a deeper warm tone than usual. I quickly recognized that as a bible verse and looked him in the eyes as I spoke to him.

"Was that from Song of Solomon?" I inquired

"It sure was. I now understand what he was feeling at that moment. That's how I feel right now as I'm looking at you".

I turned away from him nervously and barely hung on to the door as I tried to compose myself. "Man, he's laying it on thick, isn't he?" I thought as I gestured for him to come inside. Nevertheless, I liked it and I loved how he called me Darling.

"You have a lovely home." He said once he stepped inside.

"Thank you. Would you like a tour of the house? I wouldn't mind showing you. I just had it renovated not too long ago."

"I would love that." He said.

I quietly walked him around my house showing him what had been done to it and what things I didn't have changed on the home. It helped to calm me down since I was in my own space and I'm glad I offered to give him a tour. When we had finished we were back in the great room and I was grabbing my purse and light coat. Once I had everything I started walking back to him at the front door.

"I love the theme you went with for your house. I think it fits you very well."

"Thank you very much. It wasn't something I came up with on my own though. My friends greatly helped me and if it wasn't for them I would have never got this done." I told him matter of factly. I opened the door and once we were both outside I turned around to lock it.

"They did a good job. I'm currently renting an apartment about 10 minutes from here and it looks like every other apartment out there. White and like a bachelor lives in it."

"I bet your place is clean though? I get the feeling that you're a very organized person and like your house in order."

"Not really." He admitted as he opened the door for me to get into his car. I thanked him and slid into the passenger seat noting that the seats were covered in leather. He drove a 2013 silver Ford Escape which was a very smart purchase for our area. It was great on gas and handled the roads well when we had snow in the winter. It was extremely comfortable, and the interior was very clean.

"So, what you're saying is that you only clean when you have guests over but, you are a slob when nobody is around?" I asked as he backed out onto the street. Once he was on the street he turned the wheel to straighten us out and we were on our way to the museum.

"Not exactly I guess what you could say is that I'm cluttery. My bathroom and kitchen are always clean but, my living room and bedroom tend to get over run with my things from time to time." He admitted.

"I see."

"Unlike you I get the feeling that your house is always that clean. I don't think it was just because I was there today. Am I wrong?" He asked.

"Nope, you're not wrong. I laughed. I like things to always be in order. I have a type A personality as they say."

"So, if you saw my apartment you would run away screaming?"

"Depends. If you have bowls and plates of food growing penicillin in your bedroom, then yes we would have a problem." I admitted. Caius laughed a loudly and threw his head back a second to absorb the feeling. I loved to see him like that. He looked so natural and carefree. I could tell that he liked to laugh and that he loved to have fun.

"You would be happy to know that there are no scientific experiments being conducted in my apartment. To be exact my clothes and some papers from work are the only things that you would find strewn around. Is that something you can deal with?" He asked.

"Oh yea, I could work with that. My sister was far worse than that and I had to share a room with her growing up. What you have going on is nothing. It would appear Mr. Caius that you are safe pending an examination. I told him cheekingly.

"Good, now that that's settled let's get to the museum. I can't wait to see the Japanese exhibit that they have there. He said with a smile.

"I can't wait either. I don't think I have ever been there so; this will be a first for me."

"Me too? I have always wanted to go but, never did. Museums are activities you should do with other people you know? I didn't have anyone who was interested in going so, I was very surprised when you accepted this location to be our first date. You have no idea how much that meant to me."

"Your honesty is favorite refreshing Caius." I said. He chuckled.

"Are you stealing my words Ms. Sareya?" He asked me to play along.

"As a matter of fact, I am Mr. Caius. I found them to be very insightful." I admitted.

"Did you now." He said as he looked at me and then back at the road.

"Quite, Mr. Caius. Matter of fact I look forward to hearing what you have to say once we start looking at all the fine works of art."

"Me too Ms. Sareya. Me too."

$$7$$

# CHAPTER

The streets were nice and easy to drive on on the way to our destination. We parked in the parking garage and walked the last stretch of the way to the main museum doors. I had always wanted to come here but, never got the chance too. I listened to my heart beat as I beat with every step I took door the wonderful works of art I was about to view. I slid my hands on my dress. Caius turned to me and watched as I tried to rid my hands of any nervous sweat that might've formed in the last couple of minutes. He didn't say anything which I appreciated. Instead, he simply gave me a reassuring smile and began to talk to the art he had looked up online that he wanted to make sure we saw today. We walked along 38th street together toward the Indianapolis Museum of Art with the bright sun shining through the morning winter clouds. Even though the sun was hidden behind some clouds it still managed to shine magnificently despite that fact. No snow was falling and that made for no accidental falls on our first date. Thank goodness! I made sure to check the weather because I didn't want to have any accidents.

Julian paid for our tickets and we headed inside taking note of how modernized the museum looked. The outside looked like a space ship with glass windows everywhere. All them were clear blue paned and they allowed you to see outside all while hiding you away inside to look at the beautiful works of art.

"This is great architecture don't you think," he asked as we were walking toward the first group of artworks.

"It is. It almost makes you want to stay here and gaze at it without going inside any further."

He laughed at my comment and said, "We'll since we're here let's go on in, shall we?" He gently grabbed my left hand and looked me straight in my eyes. My mouth went dry and my mind went blank as the now familiar feeling started to engulf my hand again. How innocent I thought. All I wanted was for him to hold my hand forever.

I grabbed a map of the floor layout and pointed to the area we wanted to go to first. "According to the map the main exhibit we came for is this way." I said showing him so that he knew I was saying the correct information. I also wanted him to know that I could read a map very well. I was one my strong points after being taught by father as a young girl. He always relied on me to navigate on our family trips and I always took the job seriously. I'm proud to say I never got us lost.

"Alright, let's head over then." He said as he began to pull me behind him. He squeezed my hand with that action and I felt my heart skip a beat.

"Ok." I said breathlessly. I gladly followed him till we were walking side by side. I looked around the hallway and quickly saw the pic of the ballerina in the clie pose. He stopped when he noticed I had stopped moving and turned to look at it with me.

"It's beautiful isn't it?" I said thoughtlessly.

"It seems sad to me in a way."

"To me it looks like she's getting ready to go home after a long day of practice. I remember what that felt like." Caius turned to me with a smile and shocked look on his face.

"You studied ballet?" He asked with a tone of wonderment.

"Yes, and other dance styles as well." I said while reminiscing how much fun those days had been.

"Do you still dance today?"

"No. I injured my left leg in my last year of college by tearing a muscle in my knee doing a dance mover. Due to that I'm not able to do Ballet and Modern dance like I used to do. It took a year of physical therapy to heal it and another year so that I wouldn't walk with a limp. Today, I can do Jazz and other ballroom styles however so, I like to go out and dance from time to time."

He nodded his head. I could see a look of sadness on his face. It was obvious that he felt bad for me and didn't like what had happened to me. "I'm sorry to hear that. I'm glad it wasn't serious."

"Thanks." I said. Without thinking about it my eyes slowly looked down toward the floor. I can't believe I told him all of that! That's a bit too heavy on a first date Sareya! Now, I felt embarrassed. It was an accident and it happened a long time ago but, I still couldn't help feeling a bit empty. Caius's finger slid under my chin and slowly raised it back up, so I could look him in his eyes.

"I would love to take you dancing sometime. That sounds like fun. Do you know how step?" I nodded my head.

"I figured you did. I have my own little professional on my hands after all. How would you like to go to a stepper hall with me next week? We could go after dinner if you'd like?" He asked.

His finger was still under my chin but now his thumb was rubbing the side of my cheek. I closed my eyes and reveled in calmness he gave me as he touched me. It was so powerful, and it made me believe that he would take care of me without a doubt in my mind. Before I knew it the side of my face was in his hand and he continued to caress me as I submitted myself to his affection.

"You're like a cat Sareya. If you could I bet, you would purr right now." He said with a small laugh. My eyes snapped open at the sound and I quickly took my head out of his hand.

"Sorry, I didn't mean to do that." I said shakingly. My body was shaking, and I couldn't seem to get myself to calm down. How could I have done that! It probably thinks I'm crazy now! I thought as I let go of his hand to cover my face. Instantly my hand that was holding his all this time felt very cold.

"Sareya, look at me. He said as he held my face with both hands. It's ok. I liked that you felt comfortable enough to do that. Please do again whenever you want. I will gladly receive you." He said. His beautiful smile was in full view to me and he rubbed my cheeks with his thumbs as he was talking to me.

"I'm sorry. I know I must seem to be acting weird to you and…

"No need to apologize." He said. He let his hands fall back to his side and repeated the question he asked me earlier. "Would you like to go dancing with me Sareya?"

All I could do was nod my head.

"Alright, it's a date then." He reached down and took my left again and gave it a gentle squeeze. "Please, don't let go of my hand again." He said tensely. I've been thinking about holding your hand again all week. If I'm not touching you I feel like a part of me is missing somehow. I think you feel the same way too do you not?" He inquired.

My eyes grew huge at the admission that he just said to me. He feels the same way I do? I can't believe it. Then how does he seem so much calmer than I am all the time? I took a deep breath before I answered him. I wanted him to know that I felt the same way.

"Caius…" but the words wouldn't come out. Instead I smiled and tightened my grip on his hand.

"Good." He heard me loud and clear. He once again gave me a reassuring smile, turned and lead me toward the Japanese artwork exhibit.

The next couple of hours went by so quick it felt like a dream. We saw three different exhibits and looked at a variety of pre and post-world war 2 artwork from across the world. I learned that I loved the ones that were of objects and Caius loved the ones that showed movement in any type of way. It seemed fitting for him. His reflections on what he saw were dead on in my opinion too. There was one we saw with a storm brewing in colors of blue and grey mixed together with a small brown boat holding on for dear life. He explained that it made him feel empowered and by connecting it to the way he used to feel growing up as a child. Though the storm was brewing around the ship it found its way through and was heading back to the harbor. For him that was his adolescence. I found it quite profound and sad at the same time. I could only imagine what he went through. I took a moment to take a long look at the canvas.

We were almost through the museum when I became hungry but, Julian beat me to voicing it first. I laughed and told him there was a place nearby we could eat. He asked if they had steak because he loved steak and I told that I had a perfect place in mind. I got on my phone to get the address when he walked around to stand behind me. He was still holding my hand we made it point to keep this connection throughout the whole day. Good thing I was right handed. Although, according to him he didn't want to lose that connection either. With him standing behind me he was now half hugging me with my own arm and with his left arm he slowly lifted it to stroke my left cheek bone.

"Ah!" I screamed and jerked away from him. I began to heave deep breaths as if I couldn't catch my breath. My eyes became big again and the fear creeped up my back again. What was he trying to do? I thought as I reflectively contracted my hands in and out of little fists. Startled he stood still not wanting to frighten me any further. It was the first time we'd broken the connection in 3 hours.

"Are you okay? I didn't mean to frighten you." He said calmly. I heard his words and I knew he meant it but, I couldn't seem to wrap my head around the feeling. Was it sexual? No, it wasn't. I didn't want to have sex with him. Okay, that sounded bad I wanted to have sex with him but, not unless we were married. That was my pact with God and I intended on following through with that.

"Sareya, come here." Caius's voice wasn't deep nor was it high. It was a comforting medium tone and he stretched out his hand to me beckoning me to come back to him. Oh, how I wanted to. He just wanted to hug me for crying out loud! That's it. That's safe right. "Let him hold you" I heard a voice say. "It's okay, he's supposed to hold you." Oh, great now God must step in and tell me it's okay. I've really got to calm my butt down.

During my inner struggle with myself Caius once again slowly lifted his right hand and gently took a hold of my left hand. How does he know to handle me like this? Shouldn't he be running away thinking this woman's nuts?! Somehow, I immediately began to relax and all I could see was Caius's face.

"I'm so sorry Sareya, are you ok?" The look of concern on his face was very obvious to see. He wasn't scared of me. He didn't think I was crazy. He was truly worried about me. I took a deep breath to calm my nerves before I spoke to him. I didn't want to alarm him further than I already have. I'm an adult for crying out loud!

"Mmhmm. You just surprised me is all. I wasn't expecting it." I admitted.

"I won't scare you like that again. We'll go at your own pace." He said assuredly. He breathed a sigh of relief. "The last thing I want to do is make you afraid of me." Did he just say that!?

"Thank you, Caius. I appreciate that."

"Would you like to still go get some dinner with me? It's a little after 5 now and I know you must be hungry." He said. It had been over four hours since I'd eaten, and I was very hungry.

"Yes, I would love to go with you to dinner."

"Ok? He said as he looked at my face.

"Mmmhmm." I said with a small smile.

"Let's go get something to eat then. I want to learn some more about you if that's alright." I nodded my head. "Great! Now where is that restaurant you recommended that serves steaks?"

Sitting across from me at the St. Elmo Steak house was none other than Caius. We'd already eaten our meal and were now conversing about ourselves. I learned he was 24 years old and he was a native of Indianapolis. His family lived on the outskirts of the city but, he moved into the city after graduating from college. He had been offered a position during his internship and it was with the company he wanted to work with the most. He got his first pick. As a graduation gift his parents gave him the SUV that he currently drives, and they are a close-knit family. He is happily very close with his immediate family. He is one of two sons and his brother is currently a sophomore in college. He was quite accomplished academically and easily saw why they were so proud of him.

"I told my brother I paved the way for him so be better not mess it up." He said with a smirk.

"Is he serious about school like you?"

"He is, and he isn't. He's very smart and can do anything you know but, he likes to party sometimes, and it pulls him away from his studies at times. I take it upon myself to help him stay on track."

"That's nice of you."

"He doesn't see it that way. My parents worked hard for everything they have, and I don't want him to mess up the opportunities that they didn't have."

"I know what you mean. I feel the same way. My parents raised us in church and kept us focused on getting a great education. They wanted us to be able to take care of ourselves and not have to depend on anyone. I will always be thankful for that."

"How many siblings do you have? Any brothers?"

"Nope, just me and my two sisters. I took a sip my pop and wiped my face with my napkin.

"Are you from this area too?

"No, I was born in Elkhart about 3 hours north of here. I came here after I graduated from college after getting a job offer that summer.

"What did you major in" He asked. He seems genuinely interested.

"I got a degree in Health Information Technology." He sipped his pop and nodded his head.

"So, did you always want to come to Indianapolis or was it just for work?" I started messing with the rubber stopper in the back of my earring behind my ear.

"I always wanted to live in the big city so, I was excited for the opportunity. I was so happy that they offered a position shortly after graduating."

"Were you afraid you wouldn't find work? I knew I shouldn't have had any trouble finding work but, that's not the case for other students you know."

"To be honest I wasn't worried either. I got something that not only required things that I was strong in but, it was in high demand due to the new medical record laws. The dream was to have to decide between which offer I would take." I giggled remembering hoping that would happen.

"Did that happen?"

"Yea, there was a clinic at home that offered me a position at the same time I was offered this one. It was a no brainer which one to choose."

"Wow, that's a blessing."

"Yes, it was. I wouldn't change my decision at all. I love being here."

Suddenly Caius sat up straight and got an intense look on his face. For the first time I couldn't tell what he was thinking. "Are you seeing anyone else Sareya? I ask because you seem to be self-conscious whenever I touch you. Almost like you don't want anyone to see us."

My confidence drastically dissipated. I've got to tell him. If I tell him now, then we can end this with no feelings hurt. No man wants a woman like this and that's what my gut had been trying to tell me earlier in the week. It was a fear I always kept locked in the back of my mind. It was just too hard to admit to myself. Although, I prayed every day that I would meet a man that didn't have an issue with it. How in the world am I supposed to do that if I can't even act right when he tries to touch my face? I don't even know how understand the feeling I have when he holds my hand! The one thing I did know for sure was that he was really into me and I keep acting like a scared cat. I just need to tell the truth and I better tell him now. It was nice while it lasted but, I just couldn't see how he'd want to be with me after hearing this.

"No, I'm not seeing anyone but, I feel I need to tell you something important." A cold sweat and a prickly sensation began to cover my skin. My breath began to quicken, and I closed my eyes. I had to tell him. "Lord, please help him understand." I prayed. Suddenly, a calmness came over me. I opened my eyes and saw that he was holding both of my hands-on top of the table. When did he do that? I looked into his eyes and I slowly calmed down. It took a minute but then I was finally able to speak.

"I used to be a Sex Addict Caius. I was a sex addict for two years and God delivered me for three years ago. I've had 13 partners but, I was safe with every single one. I'm clean and don't have any diseases so, that's not a concern. Ever since my deliverance I've been abstinente and have not had any relationship with a man."

I looked at my hands and back at his face and saw that he was intently listening to me. There was no look of disgust on his face. Instead, he looked concerned. I kept talking.

"When I was active I would use any excuse, I could find to have sex and the men would as well. Then interesting part is I didn't enjoy it much. You would think I did because of how often I had sex but, the truth is I've never had an orgasm during sex. I did it mostly because I was looking for something and it wasn't until after my deliverance that I learned it was love that I was looking for. I wanted attention and men to adore me. Desire me and want me and at the time I thought that was how it worked. I was sadly mistaken. In the end it only caused me great pain. I knew that none of them wanted me for me but, I kept trying to think I would find him eventually. After two years of making the same mistake over and over I finally hit rock bottom. I felt so empty and I was tired of feeling this way. Going back to my foundation in Christ I picked up my bible and turned directly to a verse that spoke of coming to God when you were weary. It was then I knew I needed to make a change."

"What did you do?" He asked.

"I started going back to church at that point and asked God to take away the pain and the desire to sleep with men until I was married. I did a spiritual cleansing and fasted for 7 days. By the end of the 7 days the spirit was gone and in its place was the peace that only God could give me. It wasn't easy but, I'm glad that I did it. Now it's been three years and I have yet to experience a relationship without sex in it."

"So, you haven't been with a man in three years and haven't been in a relationship with a man in three years?"

"Nope, I haven't had a man approach me wanting to have a relationship instead of actually wanting to have sex. That's why I behaved so weird today. I apologize again."

"Sareya, you don't have to apologize for that. Now that you've explained it to me I completely understand."

"Thank you, Caius. It's just that I don't know how to breakdown the way your touch makes me feel. It does so many different things and none of them have I ever felt before." It felt like my throat was dry I stopped and took a sip of my pop.

"How does my touch make you feel Sareya?" he asked as he slowly lifted my left hand and kissed it. His lips felt so soft and warm on my skin. It was like a gentle caress with a promise of adoration attached to it.

"I love it. A lot I wish you'd never let my hand go to be honest with you. For some reason it puts me at ease and calms me down when you touch my face or my hands." He smiled and showed his perfect smile while his eyes turned into cute slits.

"Good, then I don't think we have a problem." He said as he kissed my other hand. Again, it was soft and warm. I couldn't help but believe another promise was made on my hand in less than 3 seconds. I kept looking at my hands enjoying the feel of warmth coming off them. Wait! There's no problem?

"We don't." I said flabbergasted.

"No. I don't think so." He said confidently. He kept rubbing my hands and looking at me as he spoke. For some reason it made me feel a little uneasy. It's just too good to be true.

"So, you're saying that the addiction and the number of men I was with didn't make you not want to date me? How is that even possible?" I was too shocked. Who is this guy and how could he not react in a negative way from this news?

"Well," he began to explain to me but then stopped to take a moment to think. He seemed to be transfixed by the softness of my hands. He was running his fingers along the top and the bottom of my hands.

"Soft aren't they." I stated.

"Yes…they…are. I loved the way they feel in my hands." His eyes became small again and intriguing. I loved his small eyes. When they looked at me I felt like he could see into my soul. I looked at our hands and then at his face again. He looked up then. He looked like a man who knew what he wanted, and it was obvious that he wanted me.

"The reason I don't see it being a problem is because we all have struggled with something. You went to God for help and he delivered you. I believe you when you said that because I've seen it done many times to family members and those at church. Not to mention the number doesn't bother me because let's face it many people aren't waiting to get married now a days anyway before they have sex. Nobody is perfect Sareya."

Happiness overflowed from my heart and made me want to jump up and down with joy. I couldn't believe what he was saying to me. The dress I was wearing suddenly seemed in danger of being stained from the onslaught of tears that threatened to attack at any moment. I attempted to pull my hands away to wipe my eyes but, he only let go of my right hand to do so. I grabbed my napkin and dabbed at my eyes. Good thing my makeup with waterproof.

"I'm glad I could put your fears to rest. You look like a weight has just been lifted off your shoulders." He joked.

"That's because it has." I continued to dab at my eyes. "You have no idea how scared I was to tell you this. I thought you would run screaming for the hills once you learned about my past."

"Trust me when I say. It would take a lot more to get rid of me than that." The look on his face changed to seriousness again and he grabbed both of my hands again. "I asked if you were seeing somebody because, I want to be with you Sareya. Ever since I met you I couldn't think of anything but you. You are in my thoughts day and night and you are the first thing I think of when I wake up in the morning. When I'm with you I feel complete and that's a feeling I have never felt before."

"Really? I feel the same way about you too Caius."

"To be completely honest with you I love you.

Again, for the fourth time today my eyes grew huge. At this rate they were going to fly out of my head. My jaw dropped, and my mind focused on what he just confessed to me. He loves me?

"You couldn't possibly love me already Caius. You don't even know me yet." I shook my head to emphasize my statement.

"I know some would say it's not possible but, it was love at first site for me. Would you go out with me Sareya?"

I looked down at my dress and the shoes that I had spent time and money buying for this special occasion today. This day was becoming too good to be true. Everything was out now and there was no longer any barrier preventing us from being together. So, why was I trying to create one?

"I would love to go out with you Caius. I too feel like when I'm not with you that I am incomplete. I think about you every day and wonder what you're doing. It's a foreign concept for me to be honest with you. One thing is for sure though, I want to be with you too."

"Yes! Thank you Sareya!" He lifted my hands to kiss them numerous times and we both laughed. "You have made me the happiest man in the world."

"Have I?"

"Most definitely. You are without a doubt a diamond in the rough and I was the one that was blessed to find you."

I instantly blushed and covered my face with my right hand. He reached across the table and smoothly lowered my hand from my face. My eyes were closed when I heard a small laugh come from him.

"Don't cover your face. I want to see your reactions. You're like an open book. It's so fascinating to see."

With that the last shred of self-doubt that I had vanished. This man saw me for who I really was so, I shouldn't be hiding away from him. Of course, this is easier said than done. I gave him a smile and grabbed his hand on my own this time.

"There you go. That's what I want to see." He said with a smile.

I want to too Caius. I want to too. I thought to myself. Meanwhile this entire time Caius never let go of my left hand. Our connection wasn't broken for the entire conversation.

# 8
## CHAPTER

The rain fell lightly on the suv windshield as Caius drove his car down I-465. It was a nice SUV; an ebony twilight GMC Acadia with black leather seats that felt like butter to the touch. The lights in the dashboard and the media console lit up in the dark and they began to look like a promise of things to come. Kem was playing on the radio and it made the mood even more romantic than it already was. Thankful that he couldn't see me, I smiled to myself. Today was a great day. We went to an art museum for the first time for both of us and then went to dinner at a popular steakhouse in the city. I was pleasantly full and content as Caius drove me back home.

He pulled off for the exit going to my house and I looked down to see that he was still holding my left hand. Out the passenger window street lights lit up the interior of the car as we made our way closer to my home. It had rained a couple of days before so, the streets looked a little wet. The street lights reflected off the ground and looked picturesque as they floated into the air. It was dark outside but, the moon was shining brightly in the night sky. My sister without a doubt would be taking pictures of it tonight. She loves the moon and she loves to take pictures. It just made total sense.

I turned toward him again, so I could see his profile. It was so clear, and I wanted to so badly touch his face. I wouldn't of course but, I still wanted to. His skin was so smooth and brown like a piece of my favorite chocolate. His eyes were small and as he took a quick glance at me I again felt like he could see right into my soul. It was a strong and emotional feeling. I liked it.

"Did you enjoy yourself today Sareya"? He asked as we creeped ever closer to my house. I looked out the windshield and smiled. Before I knew it, I was blushing, and I tried to cover my face.

"Don't do that. I told you, I want to see you. All of you." His words were so encouraging. What did I do to deserve this? My hand instantly fell into my lap. I couldn't help but, drop my mouth in response. Can he really see me? I'd be so happy if he could really see me! Wait, am I second guessing myself now. He stole another glance at me and answered as if he could read my mind.

"Yes, I can see you". I lowered my face. Well, that answered my question.

"I had a great time today."

"I'm very glad you did. I got a little worried that you didn't want to see me again after what I did."

"Oh no, I didn't think that at all. In fact, I'd be really upset if you hadn't tried to calm me down. I need to get used to the feelings and I'm still trying to learn how to show affection the right way."

"Worry, no more. Now that you have me everything is going to be just fine."

I believed him and for the rest of the drive enjoyed the high and focused on our hands that remained intertwined.

A short time we pulled into my driveway and Julian put the car in park. I didn't want to get out but, I knew it was time to go. I reluctantly let go of his hand and Caius walked around to open the door for me. I made sure that I had everything and got out of the SUV. I tried to prolong the inevitable by walking slowly to the front door. Of course, it didn't do much in terms of time but, I relished every second I spent in his presence. When I got to the front door he was right behind me and waited quietly while I took my keys out of my purse. Once they were in my hand I turned till I was facing him and with extreme courage gave him a kiss on the cheek. This I could do. This was ok. I wouldn't think about anything else except that I really liked this man. I had to let him know that I like him. This was the best way that I knew how.

I pulled back and looked him in his small beautiful brown eyes and smiled.

"I had a great time. Thank you so much for today. I look forward to doing it again." Caius smiled a boyish smile. Dare I say he was blushing? He touched the spot where I kissed him with his mouth open. I took my index finger and lifted his mouth back shut.

"If you leave it open like that flies will get in there. I don't think you want that." I joked. It took him a minute to realize that I was insecure anymore and caught himself in time to respond to my statement.

"I had a great time too. Can we have another date this week. I know that it's Sunday but, I really want to see you again before the weekend." I giggled happily as I listened to him speak.

"I would love that Julian. How about Tuesday? I'll be available then"? A look of triumph came over his face and he grabbed my hands.

"That would be wonderful" he said as he proceeded to kiss my hands one by one again. I couldn't believe what was happening. This man is acting as if I was a precious jewel and if he wasn't careful he'd break me. I liked it. His gaze came back up to look at me and ever so slowly leaned in to kiss me on the cheek. It felt so gentle and soothing. At the same time, I felt so precious. This is what it meant to be treasured. Caius holding my hands was also a cooling effect for me. He smelled so good and his touch was so warm but, I didn't want to sleep with him. My thoughts of him were all pure. Thank God!

"Was that ok?" He asked.

"Yes, it was very ok." A smile of triumph came across his face and squeezed my hands one last time.

"Can I call you tomorrow same time at 8pm?"

"I would like that."

"Great, until then. Have a great night Sareya."

"You too Caius. Drive safely."

With that he released my hands and started walking backwards to his car. I watched him till he got inside, and I unlocked my door. I walked across my threshold and turned to wave at him. He waved back as he pulled into the street. I heard his car tires crunch the stones in the road as he backed out into the street. He put his car in drive and then gradually pulled off. I stood there until he was out of site. Man, I missed him already.

I closed the door behind me and put my back against the door. I took out my phone and texted Shania and Luann letting them know I was home safely and walked to my bedroom.

I went through my routine of getting for bed for the next 30 minutes. I carefully unzipped my dress and took it off making sure I didn't get any makeup on it. I laid in on my dirty clothes basked and took off my shoes next. I put them up on the shoe rack and checked them to make sure there no stains that needed to be addressed first. Once I finished inspecting my shoes I went into my bathroom and turned on my shower. I didn't plan on taking a long shower. I did however want to stand under the warm stream of heat for a little while. I stepped into the shower and closed the door. I grabbed my loofa and put my favorite body wash on the spongy material. I loved this stuff and preferred it over any other brand. It not only cleaned you but, it also moisturized. During the wintertime that was pivotal.

A couple of minutes later I was finished, and I stepped out to remove the makeup on my face. I stood in front of my vanity and took out the makeup remover pads the girls gave me to remove my makeup with. It worked like a charm. I took out the facial cleanser from the same drawer and made sure to thoroughly clean my face. I turned the water to warm to rinse the cleaner off and leaned down to rinse it off my face. Now that my face was taken care of I took my electric toothbrush off the counter top and applied toothpaste to it. As a child I didn't like brushing my teeth before bed but, I made it a point to do it now that I was an adult. Besides, the electric toothbrush made it so much easier since it had a timer to let me know when I was done.

When I finished brushing my teeth I grabbed the mouthwash and within 60 seconds I was done in the bathroom. I must say this is why I didn't wear makeup every day. It added two extra steps to my day and on days when I was exhausted I was doing good making sure I put my pajamas on and made it to bed. Shoot! I was doing good if I made it to my bedroom. I walked back into my closet and walked to the side that had my dresser drawers. On the top was a bottle of lotion that matched the body wash that I just used in the shower. I made sure to use it because it was winter time and finished getting dressed. I pulled out the second drawer and selected a thin pair of pajamas that were striped with orange and yellow colors. It was quite festive. My mother bought them for me. She said that I didn't wear enough bright colors, so she took it upon herself to by me a select pair of outfits and pajamas. The shirt had long sleeves and the bottoms were a pair of pants. I didn't complain about it but, I was surprised that it bothered her the way it did. I walked out my closet and sat down on the top of my bed. I was just about to lay down and get underneath the covers when my phone starting to ring. The name on the screen said Shania. I answered the call.

"Hey Girl! How did it go!"

"It was phenomenal Shania. He was such a gentleman and we had such a great time. Hold on I have another call." I checked to see who it was. It was Luann. "Let me call you right back ok. Luann is calling. I'm going to be us on a three-way ok."

"Alright."

I hung up with her and answered the call from Luann. I told her what I was about to do and within two minutes we were all together on the line.

"So, tell us what happened? Did he try to kiss you? Shania asked. She always wanted to know about that kind of stuff first.

"On the cheek."

"What!" Shania said.

"What do you mean What? That's a good thing." Leave it to Luann to be the more reserved one.

"I'm just saying." Shania retorted.

"He kissed my hands too." I added.

"That's so sweet. How was the date itself? Did you two have a good time at the museum? I assume since you just got back that you went out to dinner as well." Luann asked.

"It went great. The museum was great, and they had many wonderful works of art. There was one part where it got kind of sketchy but, it all worked out."

"What happened?" Shania asked.

"Well, he tried to hug me and I kind of freaked out."

"You freaked out over a hug?" Shania was clearly annoyed.

"Why did that freak you out?" Luann was aware of my past so, I knew she would understand once I explained it. However, Shania didn't know anything about it. I was going to hear this in the morning.

"Since I haven't dated anyone after being delivered from my addiction I'm finding it difficult to know what's ok and what's not ok to do physically in a relationship. What seems so simple to you is not so simple for me."

"What addiction?"

"I used to be a sex addict until a little before I started working at Riley."

"You used to be a what!!!!" Yea, I was going to hear this in the morning.

"Ok, we'll get into that later. More importantly, how did he handle your reaction when he tried to hug you." Luann asked.

"He remained calm. I startled him of course but, he remained calm. He apologized to me and got me to calm down by holding my hand."

"Really?" They said in unison.

"Yea, all he did was hold my hand and I instantly began to calm down."

"Wow…that's amazing." Shania said.

"It was. I didn't know it was even possible. I thought for sure he wouldn't have wanted anything to do with me after that but, at dinner he asked me out."

"He did? What did you say" Asked Luann?

"Well, he also confessed to me that he has fallen in love with me. He said it was love at first sight."

"How romantic." Suddenly, I had Shania was on my team again.

"I told him yes and to be honest I have very strong feelings for him as well."

"What did he say when he confessed to you?" Luann inquired.

"He told me that he thinks about me day and night. When he wakes up he thinks about me and when he's not with me he feels incomplete." I was so happy to say that to my friends that I bounced up and down a couple of times.

"I want a man like that. Does he have a brother?" Shania asked.

"Yea, but, he's five years younger than you. I know you like your men older than you so, that's not going to work for you is it?"

"Man, that's not fair. Maybe I could make an exception." Shania said as she trailed off into her own thoughts.

"How was he dressed? Did he dress nicely?"

"Oh yes, he was dressed in a pair of blue jeans folded at the foot that fit his frame and a v neck brown sweater with a white shirt underneath. The sweater matched the brown that was in the blue jeans and he wore a pair of white and brown striped Adidas to bring it all together. On his head he wore an old school grey Kangoo hat that was long in the front and hugged his head in the back. Girl, you know I love those hats."

"Woah! That was very descriptive. Luann laughed.

"He also had on this really appealing cologne that wasn't loud nor too soft. It smelled very good."

"What about you? Did he liked how you looked?" Shania was back in the conversation again. I guess she gave up on trying to figure out a way to date Caius's younger brother.

"He loved how I was dressed. He even quoted a scripture to describe how I looked to him." I smiled as I thought about the way his eyes looked at me for the first time in the dress. It was an image I would never be able to get out of my head.

"He's a Christian huh? What scripture did he quote?"

"Song of Solomon 4:7 "You are altogether beautiful, my darling; there is no flaw in you.""

"Dang, that's deep." Shania replied.

"That is absolutely heartwarming for me to hear Sareya. You deserve a man like this." Luann even clapped a little bit.

"Thanks guys. I'm still reeling from it all. I even told him about my past and about my addiction at dinner. I didn't want him to think I was crazy because of the way I reacted at the museum."

"Wait a minute you told him on the first date?"

"Well yea, and even though I was nervous about telling him he took it all in and told me that everything was ok, and he still wanted to date me. He said that we all have things we have to deal with and nobody was perfect."

"Did you tell him everything or just that you an addict?"

"I mean I didn't go into any detail about what I did. I told him that I was an addict and how many men I slept with. I just felt like I needed to let him know so, he could make a good decision. I thought that was only fair for both of us. That way if he said no he would've known why I behaved the way I did earlier." The mention of him saying no made my heart hurt. I didn't like the idea of Caius not being with me. If he had told me no and that he didn't want to have a relationship it would've broken me apart.

"This man seems almost too real to be true." Luann said.

"I know that's what I thought too but, the more I listened to him and the more he reacted to me I could tell that he was serious about me. The way he looks at me is like he can see the real me. It was wonderful to finally have someone that wanted to get to know me for who I was and didn't only want to talk to me, so they could get me in bed."

"I can understand that." Said Luann.

"Me too." Said Shania.

I looked up on my wall to look at my clock that hung over my door and saw that it was almost 10pm. I told the girls that I was going to go to bed and I would talk to them later. Of course, Shania wanted to know more about what I said earlier but, I told her I'd tell her about my past at work tomorrow. She was happy with that answer and allowed me to get off the phone with no damage to my ear drums. I plugged my phone into the charger and laid it on top of my bedside table. I got into my Queen size bed and laid down absorbing the feeling of comfort and softness that covered me from head to toe. I snuggled into my sheets and my pillows making sure that I was at my most comfortable position on my side. Once I was comfortable my mind started to wander, and I thought over what a great date this was. I couldn't deny that I enjoyed his company and I certainly couldn't deny that he really liked me. He wore his heart on his sleeve so, it was easy to tell how he was feeling. I liked that about Caius and I believed that he did love me.

I've known people in my own life that fell in love at first sight and even got married within a month of meeting each. They are still married to this day. I know of another couple that fell in love at first sight and they got married within a year of meeting. They are also still married to this day. I knew very well that it was possible. I was the romantic type and I dreamt of finding a man that would fall me instantly. I must admit though that seeing it happening was unsettling at first. The more I thought about though I was comforted by the thought. He loves me. "Caius loves me!!!" I exclaimed out loud.

Where would we go from here I wonder? I know we're going to go out on another date on Tuesday evening. I couldn't wait for that. I wonder if he was thinking of taking me dancing or not? If he does I would have to make sure I wore the right outfit. Not saying that I wouldn't wear something nice for any of our dates but, there was something to be said about the one you wear when you go dancing with someone you like. You don't want to wear anything to tight, too revealing, short, or to big. You also wanted to dress for the temperature of the location and not the weather outside. This applies unless the dance even was outside of course.

I wanted to make sure that I picked out an outfit that was comfortable, airy, and fit my body type. In my case I also had to have no sleeves just like I did tonight. I would most likely be sweating whenever I go dancing. Being able to breath in my clothes was extremely important. I already had dance shoes that I would wear so, that wasn't even a concern. I got up out of my bed so, that I could pick out my dance outfit early. With this being a part of my personality there was no way I couldn't have this already ready to go. The floor was cold underneath my feet as I walked back into my closet. The closet was covered in carpet so, I got a reprieve from the cold for the time being.

I started to go rifle through my hangers and looked through the dresses that kept the dance outfits all together. I went through it article of dance clothing till I got near the end and a red sleeveless halter dress that came down to my knees showed up. It was made of cotton and came with a pair of leggings that went down to your knees. It was perfect. I hung it on the hook on the left side of the bathroom door so, I could just grab it when it was time to get ready. Now that my outfit for my date on Tuesday was picked out my brain would be able to relax. I walked back to my bed and slid back underneath the covers. My feet were cold while I tried to get them to adjust to the heat in the blanket. Maybe I should just wear socks to bed again. I turned to my right side and nestled back into the pillows the way that I had just done a couple a little while ago. The sheets were so soft, and the blanket covered me as I started to unwind from the day that I had.

It was a long day. I spent the day with my girls and they helped me get ready for this date and for that I would be forever grateful. The rest of the day was spent with Caius and I would never forget this date for as long as I lived! He was so much fun to be around, and he was so smart. I was happy to hear about his family and how he valued getting good education like I did. I enjoyed his laugh and I loved his smile. He was someone I could easily see myself with. I turned myself onto my back and looked up to look at my ceiling light. It was off, and my bedside table lamp was the only light on in the bedroom. I missed him already. I thought. I wonder if he's asleep yet.

I hugged my pillow and kicked my feet as the feeling of euphoria washed over me. I've never had a man tell me he loved me before. I've also never had such strong man be able to handle my situation so well.

He was such an amazing man. He was handsome and to top it all off he was a Christian. I liked that he had a take charge side to him as well as a compassionate side. I liked it when he was near me and I liked the sound of his voice. I loved that he held my hand the entire day. I liked it when he took my feelings in consideration to make sure that he did not scare me. Learning that having that connection was as important to him and it was to me was mind boggling. I...I.... I really liked him. I really liked him.

# 9
# CHAPTER

The wind feels warm on my face as I'm walking from my car to my parent's front door. The weather was sunny and bright, and I couldn't wait to see my family after being away for a couple of months. My nephew runs out of the house and gives me the biggest hug that I have ever received from him to date.

"Hi, Aunty Sareya! "His arms wrap around me and he squeezes me as hard as he can. The feel like happy.

"Hi, nephew. How are you? Have you been a good boy?" I release him, and he continues to keep his grasp on me. /I know he never likes to let me go so, I just stand as he's holding on.

"I'm good. I turned 6 today!" He says with excitement. I smile and rub his back as I continue my walk to the front door.

"I know. That's why I'm here. Today's your birthday party." He looks at me with this big toothless smile on his face.

"Mmhmm and we're about to start. Your just in time." I open the door and inside I see my entire family. They were all gathered in the living room and my nephew's friends were running amuck within the home.

"Oh, thank goodness you're here.!" My sister said with a huge sigh of relief. She looked nice but, she was a little bit stressed.

"Hi, Victoria. Do you need any help?" She grabs my harm and hurls me into the kitchen without another word. Once inside of the kitchen she puts both of her hands on my shoulders.

"Sareya, is everything ok with you?" She sounds very concerned.

"Yea, why do you ask?"

"I heard about your "activities" is anything about it true?" She asked. She turned and put her hands on her hips. I could tell she didn't believe me. My parents came into the kitchen at this point and took a seat at the kitchen table.

"Mom, she said it isn't true." My mother breathed a sigh of relief.

"So, what Mrs. Wallace said wasn't true." My mother inquired.

"What did she say mom." I asked thoroughly confused.

"Well, she said that she saw you with many men lately. What have you been doing with them?" Suddenly, my breath caught in my throat. Mrs. Wallace lives near my school and she must have seen me around. My family has now found out my secret.

I hadn't responded for a couple of seconds when my father jumped into the conversation.

"Just tell us the truth Sareya. What's been going on?"

I sat up quick in my bed and the coolness of the bedroom air was sucked into my lungs. I looked around and saw that it was still dark out. I continued to breathe heavy and I squeezed the blanket in my hands. I looked at my hands and told myself to relax. It was just a dream after all. It was one of my biggest fears but, it was a dream no less.

"How many times am I going to have these dreams." I thought to myself. It had to have been. It's the only thing that I've been fearful of in the last couple of years. It was hard to pinpoint because most of the time I didn't remember them. The ones I did remember were done just like this. I haven't been able to tell my family that I was once a sex addict. As supportive as they are I did not think that they would be able to handle something like this. I wasn't raised to do something like that and to hear that I had I felt would break my parents heart. I knew that they would be proud of the fact that I went to God for help and that I was delivered but, it still didn't feel like I could tell them why I did it. I wasn't afraid they would disown me or anything. I also didn't feel that they would hate me. I was more afraid of them being disappointed in me. I can't tell them yet. Not until I get engaged. I felt like when I did that my family would be comforted in knowing that I found someone that loved me and wanted to marry me despite my past. I had heard how hard it was to find someone with a past like mine. I refused to believe that I wouldn't find anyone because, I had God looking for me. I knew I would find him soon and then I would tell them. I can't tell them. I just can't tell them now. At least not yet.

It was 7:55 am when I walked onto my floor and was making my way to the break room when Shania came out of nowhere to bum rush me.

"Morning, Sareya! How are you feeling today?" She was smiling ear to ear. No doubt she was happy to hear about my date last night.

"I'm good." I decided not to tell her about the dream last night. I wanted to see what would happen after I told her about my past first before I told her about the nightmares. I didn't want to confuse here.

I walked into the break room and made my lemon tea. It tasted delicious and as soon as I finished it Shania hooked her arm in mine and dragged me into my office. Good thing my mug was nice and high.

"Man, Shania can I finish preparing my tea before you drag me around."

"No, I need to hear what you promised to tell me today. You promised." We had just set foot into my office when I heard a very familiar voice behind me.

"What did you promise to tell her?" It was Eli. I had forgotten that he would be back today. He had texted me last week to let me know he was doing ok after his outpatient surgery. I knew he was doing well but, somehow, I forgot that he would be back today. The vacation was over. He was very protective of me and he looked out for me since our days in high school. We have always been great friends and he was the one I ran to whenever I needed help with anything. We never dated though.

"Hmm?" My eyes were big, and I remembered that he was the only one who knew what happened back then. He and I went to college together and he watched out for me. He was then and still is my best friend. However, he felt it was something I didn't need to tell anyone except my future husband. He probably wouldn't like the fact that I'm about to tell Shania. He stared at me with his famous "You know I know you better than anyone so, I know your lying right now" look.

"Don't worry about it Eli. It's just girl talk."

"Is it now" He said with a smirk on his face. I'm surprised that Shania hasn't tried to get with Eli because, I thought that they would be a good match for each other. He looked at Shania and then turned to look at me. I finally cracked under the pressure.

"Come in Eli. You can be my witness." I pushed him into my office and closed my door. I made my way back to my chair and we all sat down at the same time.

"What's going on Sareya? Did something happen while I was gone?" He asked. Quickly his voice went from playful to concerned.

"Nothing happened here. This is about me."

"What's happened with you? Are you sick?" His eyes were now big at this point.

"No, calm down Eli. I'm fine." Shania then took this opportunity to join in the conversation. Everyone in the department knew that he and I were great friends.

"Actually, she's more than fine. She has a new boyfriend!" She clapped her hands in excitement. Eli's eyes stayed huge.

"You do?" He looked at me with a confused look on his face.

"Yea, and they went on their first date yesterday and she said it went beautifully! OOOOO, I'm so happy for her. She has been single for far too long. I was beginning to think that she was never going to find anyone."

Eli looked upset.

"Um, Shania. Could you give me and Eli a second?"

"What?! You said you would tell me today."

"I will. I will tell you at lunch ok?"

"Alright, I'll come get you at 11:58. Make sure you are ready."

She stood up and walked out of the office. My eyes watched as the door closed behind her and then my eyes made contact with Eli's again. He was not happy. He had his arms crossed and the expression on his face now read "You better tell me everything". He has never had to say much to get his point across to me.

"Let me start by saying I am very sorry."

"Thanks, and your forgiven. Now you have a boyfriend now?"

"Yea." It felt good to say that.

"And when did this happen?"

"Last Monday." He liked short answers whenever he was interrogating me. Afterwards I could explain all I wanted.

"And you had your first date yesterday?"

"Yes." Once again it felt good to say that. I wondered if Caius had anyone interrogating him about me? Eli relaxed his shoulders and uncrossed his arms. He leaned forward in his seat and put his right hand on his chin.

"Tell me about him?"

"Well, his name is Caius Locke and no you don't know him. He's from here. He is 23 years old, he works in Cyber Security, he drives a GMC Arcadia, and he is a Christian. He said nothing. "I have a picture of him if you want to see what he looks like."

"Ok. He has a stable job, he has his own car, and he's a Christian. Good to know. Was he respectful? Was he appropriate?".

"Yes, he was." I didn't want to tell him about how Caius tried to hug me. He would take that out of proportion.

"Good. When do I get to meet him?"

"Woah! Can we go on a couple of more dates before I introduce him to you?"

"Why?"

"Because... I want to make sure he's permanent before I introduce him to anyone."

"Fine, you have two more dates but, then I get to meet him. More importantly, how come you didn't tell me about him in the first place? What are you so afraid of?"

"You know how you can be Eli. Nobody is good enough for me and I was afraid that you would scare him away. I appreciate that you look out for me so, please trust that I am making a good decision without you this time."

He lowered his head and thought about it for a minute. I sat there quietly while I waited. I knew asking this of him was a huge request. While I waited I thought about him meeting Caius. Over all I thought that they would most likely get along but, I didn't want them to meet too soon. I wasn't sure how Caius would take me having make friends and I wasn't sure what he would think about me working with Eli as well.

"Alright. Just do me a huge favor and keep me updated ok. I just want to make sure he is not taking advantage of you. You and I both know what happened before."

I nodded my head. "Yes, I do. I've learned since that time and now know what to look out for. Don't worry. I have everything under control." I stood up and walked till I was standing on the side of my desk. "Please trust me ok?" I will always be grateful to Eli for watching over me. It was also because of him that I went back to church and got delivered in the first place. He was there when I hit rock bottom and pulled me back on my feet. He was the one who encouraged me saying that I didn't have to stay this way and that with the Lord's help I could change.

He stood up and pulled me into a tight hug. "Be careful Sareya. If you need me, I'll always be right here ok? "He gave me a sweet kiss on my forehead and then pulled away to look me in the eyes. According to him he could always tell that I was lying by looking into my eyes.

"I will. Thanks Eli. I can't wait for you to meet him." Apparently, what he saw passed the test.

"I'll be heading to my office then. They'll be a meeting at 3pm today about the new policy changes with the email accounts so, make sure your there on time ok." He laughed and quickly walked out of the door.

"Why do you always have to bring up that up. I was late one time!" I yelled as he walked out of my office.

"Because you know it's true." He said as he stuck his head back in my office door.

"Get out of here. I'll see you at the meeting." I said as I closed the door on his face. He just laughed and walked down the hallway. I could hear him as he made his way all the way back to his office on the other side of the department floor.

I walked back to my desk chair laughing at my friend. I couldn't wait till he met Caius.

# 10
# CHAPTER

It was 11:58 am and as if on cue I looked up from my computer screen and there was Shania standing in the doorway. Luckily, I already had my coat on and my purse ready to go and I was simply waiting for her. I stood up and began to walk to the door before she even uttered a word.

"Wow, your ready huh?"

"Sure am. Where are we headed today?" I said as I walked past her and out to the elevator.

"How about soups sandwiches today? I'm craving breads today and there is a small restaurant nearby that has great soups and salads."

"Cool, let's go."

Before long we were standing in line waiting to order our lunch. It was a small shop with a few tables for sitting inside and a few tables for sitting in the front of the shop. Since it was cold there wasn't anyone sitting outside but, there also wasn't that many people at the standing tables either. It seems that many took their food to go which worked out for us. The floor was a glazed factory stone floor and the walls were made of red brick. On the walls were 1930's posters. The ceiling was open with lights hanging from the wood beams. It was an industrial feel and quite creative in my opinion. The line moved fast and in less of a minute we were at the front and placing our orders. I asked for the ½ turkey sandwich on wheat bread with mayonnaise, mustard, ketchup, and pickles, and american cheese. For my soup I asked for the spicy vegetable soup. I went to the end of the line and watched as they made my sandwich right before my eyes. The food looked delicious and I couldn't wait to get it on my own tray. Shania was right behind once she ordered her food and waited with me at the end of the line. We paid for our lunch and right after we finished paying our food was ready. I didn't realize how hungry I was till I walked in the restaurant. I was starving!

We walked to the table right in front of the window and happily sat down to eat our lunch. It looked delicious. I took out my hand sanitizer, we cleaned our hands, and then we prayed over our food. As I finished my prayer I lifted my sandwich to my mouth to taste first. The soup was still too hot for me to try yet. Once the sandwich touched my tongue all I could think about was how was exquisite it was. I was definitely going to come back here again, and I hadn't even tried the soup yet. After a few bites and our bellies filling back up Shania began to start her questioning again.

"So, what was it that you were going to tell me about your past?" I took sip of my lemonade and mentally prepared myself to tell her the truth.

"Remember why you asked me why I stopped hanging out with you out to the clubs? It was because I used to be a Sex addict."

She stopped eating her food and put her sandwich back down. "You were a sex addict."

"Yes. It was during college and I when I came here I had just started to be abstinent. It got old trying to keep the guys away from me when all they wanted was one thing. To avoid all of that I just decided to stop going out like that. I'm sorry if I hurt your feelings. I never intended to."

"Are you still struggling with it now?"

"No."

"How is that?" I explained to her what I did, and she was amazed at my story. Being one that went to church sometimes she found it very enlightening. She'd never heard about spiritual cleansing delivering someone from a sex addiction.

"Ever since that day I haven't had any problems with it. I am however having a little trouble figuring out what is ok as far as touching goes when it comes to dating again. That's why during the date it was so weird to finally hold someone's hand and I felt really calm. Before it wasn't like that.

I used to think about sexual things whenever I would touch a man or see a man that I thought looked good."

"I get it. I'm so sorry Sareya. Is there anything I can do?"

"Girl, no. Just listen to me and help me understand if what I'm feeling was right or if I was simply overreacting."

She grabbed my hand and gave it a gentle squeeze. "I am here for you Sareya. Talk to me anytime. I will be there for you."

"Thanks Shania."

We continued to eat our lunch and we talked about her love life for a little while. Apparently, she had a guy that she started seeing that she was kind of crazy about. I was very happy for her. I took a sip of my soup for the first time and it was heavenly. She thought so too and before we knew it our soups were gone. I would have to get this to eat again.

"So, tell me. How did you meet him?"

"Oh, at the grocery store."

"At the grocery store?"

Yea, I was in the cereal aisle when this handsome man walked by and asked me if I knew where the Frosted Flakes were."

"He did? When was this?"

"A couple of weeks ago. He wasn't serious of course. He was just trying to get my attention. He looked really nice so, I showed him where the cereal was that we were looking for."

"Then what happened?"

"Well, he thanked me and asked me if I was seeing anybody."

"My goodness. That was kind of sudden wasn't it?"

"Not really Sareya. You have been out of the game for so long that you don't know how it works anymore."

We both laughed uncontrollably at that statement. She was right. How would I know?

"So, you told him you were single then?"

"Yep, and he asked me out for a date. We went out that weekend and we've been seeing each other ever since. Oh, by the way his name is Troy." She smiled and took a sip of her lemonade.

"That's awesome Shania! I'm so happy for you." She showed me a picture on her phone and I agreed with her that he was a very handsome guy.

"He's a gentleman too girl. He holds doors open for me, he isn't aggressive with me because you know I can't deal with that. I don't want to have a man who feels he needs to be controlling and possessive."

"I agree with you about that. The last thing I need is a man telling me what to do or asking me why I didn't answer his phone calls when he calls me."

"Isn't that the truth. Caius isn't like that either then I take it."

"No, every time I've talked to him during on date he was not possessive or controlling at all. If anything, he was more about me taking my time and understanding of my situation. However, I also know that he is very aggressive when he wants to be. It's nice because I like the fact that he lets me know how much he likes me, and he is not afraid to tell me what he thinks and how he feels."

"That's great girl. Troy and Caius should me each other soon. You know like a double date. She clapped her and squealed in her trademark way that I've come to know and love.

"I agree with you. Who knows we might even become "Couple friends". I said with a goofy look on my face. I knew that she would love that idea more than anything else in the world when it comes to us.

"Oh yea! That would be excellent. We would be together all the time like the couples on tv."

I looked at my clock while Shania did another squeal and I saw that it was almost 12:45am. We were only 10 minutes away from the hospital so, I told her let's head on back. I didn't want us to be late. How would that look with us being the manager and the assistant managers being late.

"Ok. Let's go. I'm nice and full. I will be ok through the rest of the day."

"Me too."

On my way back home from work all I could think about was talking to Caius. I wanted to share with him the new things that I went through today. To know that my friends were all supportive and that they all knew the truth was like a huge weight being lifted off me. My shoulders felt lighter and feet felt peppier as I walked into my house. I changed my clothes and went back into the kitchen to make myself some dinner. I was craving something with rice and chicken so, I made myself some lemon pepper chicken and yellow rice meal with an apple and cranberry salad. I was about to finish cooking my dinner when my cell phone rang.

I leaned behind me over the peninsula and grabbed my cell phone. I slid the phone answer bar to the right and put the phone on speakerphone. I knew better than to hold it up to my ear. I've almost dropped my phone too many times in the food while I was cooking.

"Hello?"

"Hi kitten. How are you?"

"Kitten? Who is that?" I smiled to myself.

"I know your smiling. I can hear it over the phone."

I giggled and proceeded to put the food on my plate. I made plenty for another person so, I'll just save it to eat tomorrow.

"Well, so what if I am?"

"That's the reaction that I want. Never stop smiling ok?"

Man, I love how this man makes me feel. I feel so good about myself and I can't help but smile when he's talking to me.

"Did you have a good day today?" At this point my food was ready to eat. I took the chicken out of the skillet and the rice and laid it on my porcelain plate. The food emitted a mouthwatering aroma and I could hear my stomach rumble. I carried my plate to the table and had a seat. I hadn't eaten since lunch so, I was famished.

"I did. I told my friends that I was officially off the market and they were not exactly happy about it."

"They weren't happy that I took you off the market huh?"

"I wouldn't say that. It was more like they were concerned about the way I was handling things since it'd been a long time."

I wasn't quite sure about telling him about Eli quite yet. I knew that some men had a problem with their woman having a close male friend so, I wanted to feel him out before I told him about him. I mean we had just started dating so, there was no way that I would know how he felt about that sort of thing.

"I don't blame them. I would be concerned too if you were my best friend." Oh, this sounded like that perfect opportunity for me to tell him now. I think I will take that chance.

"Yea, my friend Eli was very worried about me. We have been friends since high school and we also work together."

"He sounds like a really nice guy."

"Yea, he is. He's been there through it all. He's like a big brother to me."

I swear I could feel the relief fall off his chest. Although it could have just been my imagination.

"I'm glad you had someone to take care of you during that time. I hope that the more we get to know each other that you would start to allow me to be there for you too."

"We will see Mr. Locke." I smiled to myself. How was your day today? Are you guys going to be ending the workshop soon for the new program?"

A huge sigh of relief came out of his mouth and I could tell he was smiling on the other end of the phone.

"Yes, thank goodness. It's been a long-awaited ending. The last day will be this Friday."

"I can tell that you want to celebrate the moment the last class ends."

"You're dern tootin!" I chuckled to myself. I took a bite of my food and let the chicken melt into my mouth. It was mouthwatering. Unknowingly, I must have given off a loud "mmmm" because Caius made sure to comment on it.

"Sounds like whatever you are eating tastes really good. What are you eating?"

"Lemon Pepper Chicken with yellow rice and apple salad."

"That does sound good. I understand now why you are enjoying the meal."

"I'm sorry if I am loud. Are you eating? Have you eaten yet?"

"I haven't eaten yet but, I doubt what I have will be anywhere close to what you are eating." I giggled as I took another bite of my food.

"Do you cook Caius?"

"I do. My father taught me when I was a little boy. He always enjoyed creating meals."

"Do you share in the same love for cooking or are you more like you cook for survival?"

"I would say that I'm half of each. There are days I like to create things out of nothing and there are times when I like to just heat up some soup and sit down after a long day of work."

I laughed so hard I almost chocked on my food. "I can cook very well but, I only do it because I have to. I prefer to bake over cooking. When I bake it gets my blood racing and I can't wait to see the result after making a cake, pie, or cookies."

"You like to make all of those things huh?"

A slow smile spread across my face at the sound of his voice. It felt so warm and curious. I loved the fact that he wanted to know more about me. I loved that he wanted to hear more about myself and what I had to say.

"I really do. From what you told me. It sounds like we should have a dinner date where we cook together sometime. You would make the dinner and I would make the dessert. I have no doubt that it would taste delicious."

"I bet it would too. How about we do that this weekend?"

"I would be more than happy to taste the food that you make."

"Me too. I can get the ingredients together by then. How about this Saturday night?"

"Sounds good to me. What would you like for me to make?"

"Can you make a white lasagna? It was one of my favorite dishes. If you can make that then I will make a strawberry tart to go along with it for dessert."

"Mmmm, that sounds absolutely perfect. Where do you want to have the dinner date? My apartment is smaller than your house and my kitchen isn't as big as yours either. How about we do it at your house?"

"How about we have it at my house this time and then at your house next time?"

"It's a date."

"Alright, meet me at my house on Saturday at 2pm. Bring your groceries and we will make our first dinner together. I am so excited now!" I was so happy that I found myself putting down my phone, putting it on speaker and clapping my hands in anticipation.

"Excited, aren't you? I am excited too. I have never done anything like this before. Have you?"

"Nope. It is something that I have dreamt about before. It was something that I read about a lot but, I didn't think it would ever happen to me."

"You deserve the best Sareya. I am happy to know that I will be the first person that has a dinner date with you and make food in your kitchen."

"Well, that's only because I just had the kitchen finished in the last couple of weeks." I giggled.

"Still I will be the first and hopefully I will be the last."

"You keep getting a good score card then you just might be."

"I have a score card? Like a report card from school? That is messed up." He laughed.

"It's not as bad as you think but, I thought I heard what you said. You know about having a woman that doesn't speak her mind, right?

"Yea, that's true."

"Well, then I'm pretty sure that you have some sort of score card for me as well."

"You really analyze things, thoroughly don't you?"

"Oh, you have no idea."

# 11
## CHAPTER

I picked out a shopping cart while Luann waited for me patiently. It wasn't as busy that evening thankfully while I was out doing my grocery shopping. I put my things in the seat of the cart and proceeded to walk toward the milk aisle. I wanted to get the ingredients that I needed for the dinner that I was going to make with Caius. Today was Friday and I wanted to make sure that I had fresh ingredients for our date tomorrow.

"Ok, what are we getting tonight." She asked as she picked up a gallon of orange juice.

"I need some tart shells, apple juice, cornstarch, white sugar, and fresh strawberries. I don't want to get anything frozen. I'm doing this tomorrow so; I have to make sure everything I get is top quality."

"Alright, Rachel Ray. I will make sure I don't get anything that is not fresh."

"Hey, don't make fun of me. You know if it were you it would be the same way."

"Fine, your absolutely right about that. I would probably not even try cooking anything and would simply order my food from a fancy restaurant."

"Wait a minute, you are telling me instead of cooking for your man you would buy a dinner and then pass it off as your own?"

"I sure would, and I wouldn't be ashamed about it either." Luann grabbed a container of the dough for me and continued to make her way to the juice aisle.

"I am just saying that I can't believe you would deceive your man like that. I don't feel that it's even necessary. If you are just concerned over the fact you can't cook that well, then never offer to cook for him. That's a lot easier don't you think?"

"Geez Sareya! I'm just saying that not all of us can cook like you so, we must come up with other ways to appease our men in that department. You know they still want us to do all of the cooking!"

I grabbed a 64 oz container of apple juice and continued my way to the next aisle.

"I don't agree that all men want us to cook. To be exact I think that many men don't feel that way anymore. Instead I think some prefer to eat out most of the time."

"Wow, you are completely disillusioned, aren't you?"

"On the contrary. I'm an optimist."

"Well, Ms Optimist I hear what you're saying, and I won't trick a man into thinking that I cooked a meal that I bought at a fancy restaurant. Instead, I'll just tell him I don't cook, and we'll eat out all the time."

"You could just learn to cook Luanne." I said as we walked into the produce aisle.

"Last time I checked you didn't like to cook either."

"No, I didn't but, after moving here I had to learn. I didn't want to live off fast food. Once I started I found out that I was really good at it."

"Well, I tried it and I'm not so, I'm never going to cook for my man."

"Ok, you could at least make a crockpot meal can't you."

"Crockpot meals? What in the world is that?"

"Before I get any further, do you even know what a crockpot is?"

"Yes, it's the thing that cooks food for you that my mother uses every holiday season."

"Great! Well, the beauty of the crockpot is all you have to do is pour your ingredients into it before you leave for work and by the time you get home it'll be ready for you to eat."

"Are you serious? There is a kitchen appliance that actually cooks food while I'm gone and won't burn the house down?" I couldn't help but, laugh at her statement. I almost dropped the strawberries I was inspecting because I was laughing too hard.

"Yes, and women all over the world love it. You should get a cookbook on crockpot recipes and use that to make a meal for your man at least one time."

"Fine Sareya, I'll do that. However, I don't even know why we are talking about a man that doesn't even exist anyway"

"That's because you do not want to wait until you have a man to work on this type of thing."

Luann turned to the apples and it looked like she was thinking hard.

"Look Luann I am just trying to help you. You can take the advice, or you can leave it. I'm just saying that you are very capable of doing it so, at least try. Don't you want him to see what your fully capable of."

She slowly turned back to me and gave me a look of acceptance. I put the strawberries I selected in the cart and spread my arms open for her.

"I got it." She took a deep sigh. "How you go with me to the store to get a recipe book and help me make my first meal."

"I would love too."

"Do we have everything we need now?"

"Yes, I believe so."

"Good, can we go back get some things for my house? I'm out of groceries for my house."

No problem. Matter of fact how about I look on the recipe app I have and look up some recipes for you to start with for your crockpot?"

"Sure, while we're at it we also need to buy a crockpot."

It was 5:00 in the evening and I was expecting Caius in the next 30 minutes. I had my kitchen nice and clean and I had all the ingredients just waiting to be brought out. I was wearing a purple short sleeve shirt with denim distressed skinny jeans. Knowing that I would be nervous I made sure to wear something that was breathable. I was working on my makeup in my bathroom while I was waiting for him. I had Pandora on the relaxation music station so, I could get ready while getting ready in the bathroom. I decided to go with a natural look with a glimmery lip gloss that Shania gave me to try. It had a hint of red in it but, it wasn't over that top.

I couldn't wait to see him and thought about how we have talked everyday this past week. He makes me feel good about myself and I couldn't wait to talk to him again. He's so supportive and understanding that I was afraid to see what was wrong with the man. I mean let's face it, nobody was perfect. I got the feeling though that I would be able to handle it though. Relationships are about give and take and no relationship is perfect. For some reason when I was younger I thought that there was such a thing as an all-sunshine and rainbow relationship. I now know that that is not even possible, and we need to accept people for all their flaws. My fear was that I wouldn't find anyone who would accept mine.

I walked out into the living room and put the tv on the food channel. It was always a good way of distracting myself and a way to get me in the mood to cook when I was tired. I looked at the clock on the cable box and the time read 5:15pm. I had gone and got a pedicure yesterday after Luann and I left the grocery store. It was great hanging out with her. We went to my favorite shop that I frequented once a month and she wanted to see if she would like it herself. She did, and she wanted to come back with me next month. I was still getting used to the fact that my best friend was close to me and we could hang out whenever we wanted to.

I felt beautiful and at the same time was very nervous. I thought doing this in my kitchen would help me feel more comfortable. I hoped this worked. Any second now I was about to hear my doorbell ring and he would be standing at my door. I couldn't wait to see what he was wearing. He always dressed so nice and I wondered if he would since we were cooking this time. I imagined that he would dress comfortably but, still be dashing.

I was watching the front window facing the yard and the street. I couldn't wait to see him pull up and walk up to my front door. I heard my phone notification go off to let me know that I received a text message. Glancing at it momentarily I saw that it was Luann and right after hers came through Shania's appeared at the top of my screen. I shook my head in defeat because I realized after reading their messages that they didn't trust that I could get through this date on my own. Shania was worried that I would crack under the pressure of having him in my house. I honestly didn't think that I would have that problem but, I liked the fact that she was concerned. Luann was simply worried period that I didn't want to be alone. I quickly returned their texts letting them know that everything is fine, and they didn't need to worry about me.

As soon as I finished my texts my doorbell rang, and I nearly jumped out of my seat. I was severely disappointed. I wanted to see him pull up but, it's ok. I was certain that it wouldn't be the only opportunity to see it. Rushing to the front door I opened it to reveal Caius standing on my doorstep. He looked amazing. He was wearing a thin black long sleeve sweater with a pair of slim cut blue jeans.

"Hi, kitten. How are you today?" He asked. He was carrying two plastic bags of groceries in one hand and in the other hand ½ a gallon of apple cider.

"Hi Caius." I said sweetly. "I'm doing good. Come on in. The kitchen is this way." I lead the way into the kitchen. "You could lay your groceries right there on the island." He set his groceries down and then turned to face me.

"You look beautiful today Sareya."

"Thank you, Caius. You do as well." I said. I know the smile on my face was really goofy.

"If you don't mind I'm going to put some music on while we cook. I like to cook with music on. Is that ok?"

"Sure. I don't mind. Do whatever you need to to feel comfortable."

"Thanks." I turned the music on my phone and walked to the refrigerator to take out the cold ingredients for my strawberry tarts.

"Is it ok if I use this side of the island." He asked as we took out everything out of the bags.

"Sure. I don't mind working on this side." I gestured to the oven and asked him what temperature he needed to set it on. Once he told me the temperature I walked over to the oven and reached to turn it on. When I did I accidentally bumped my hand into his reaching to set the temperature as well. I felt an electric current migrate its way from my hand all the way to the top of my head. It shook me up for a second and I smiled with a feeling of shock and surprise.

"Did you feel that too?" He asked with a shaky voice. His eyes were alert and staring me right in my eyes. I nodded my head and rubbed my hands on my pants.

"Sareya…." He said my name and it hung in the air for a couple of seconds. The music continued to play in the background as I waited to hear the rest of what he had to say. He raised the hand that touched mine and placed it on the counter.

"May I kiss you?"

My mind registered what he asked me but, I couldn't believe that he asked me. I would be lying if I didn't want him to though. It's a feeling I hadn't felt for a couple of years. I was looking forward to it.

"Yes."

He placed his right hand that had just touched me and placed it on the left side of my cheek. His palm felt warm and tender. I placed my left hand on his out of instinct and felt how warm his hand felt under my own. He was naturally warmer than me and I liked it. He stepped gingerly towards me and placed his left hand on my right cheek. As he leaned in, I closed my eyes and anxiously waited for him to kiss me. The very next moment I felt his lips on mine. They were soft. In the next moment I felt that same electric current from before traveling its way from my lips to the back of my head. We immediately pulled apart and looked at each other with our mouths open in a "o" shape. At this rate I was beginning to think that we wouldn't ever be able to touch or even kiss each other. This was beginning to get ridiculous.

"Woah."

"Yeah." I responded breathlessly. Surprisingly enough I wasn't timid or scared. Only shocked a bit.

"Can I kiss you again." He asked with a boyish smile on his face.

"I don't know. I'm scared to see what happens if you kiss me again."

He laughed and asked me again.

"May I please kiss you again Sareya?"

"Your trying to kill me, aren't you?" I laughed as I shook my head.

"What you felt was what many look for all the time. You know, Chemistry." He said with a smirk. I laughed hard at his statement. He wasn't wrong. This was what many people kept looking for in their relationships. I knew for a fact that if there wasn't any chemistry many would end the first date in the first five minutes. Even worse they would end the very first conversation in the first five seconds. He was now giving me side look with a smile patiently waiting for me to give him an answer.

"Ok. You can kiss me again." As soon as I said that you would have thought that the man had won a million dollars. It felt good to see that he valued me so highly. That's the kind of man I had been waiting for. He placed his hands lightly on my face. I loved it when he gently pulled me toward him. I closed my eyes again as he leaned in to kiss me. His lips pressed against me again and I moaned from the feeling. This time he stayed connected to me despite the chemistry that occurred. It felt so good. I was very happy that he asked to kiss me again. It was a chaste kiss and it said so much to me in ways I never thought possible. He pulled away from me slowly and I opened my eyes. I couldn't wait to do it again.

"Hmmm." He said murmuring under his breath. My thoughts exactly. I took a step back and slowly shook my head in disbelief. This kiss was perfect.

"Thank you, Caius."

"Oh no kitten. Thank you." His look turned to concern for a moment and I could tell that he had a question. He must have warred over asking me or not because, his eyes slowly shifted back to happiness. He must not have wanted to know after all. I could only think that the question had to deal with my past. He said it didn't matter but, I knew I should be honest if he ever asked any questions.

"I wanted to let you know that was the best kiss I've ever received. I have never felt that before."

"I can honestly say that I haven't felt anything like that before either. It is definitely the best kiss I have ever received too."

I couldn't help but, smile to myself. He was smiling too, and I could tell that he was proud of himself.

"We should get started cooking Caius." I enjoyed saying his name. It flowed right off my tongue.

"Your right kitten." He slowly lowered his hands from my face. You could tell that he was reluctant to do it. He only did it because I asked him too.

It was 7 o'clock when we had finished making our meals and I was now sitting at my dinner table waiting for the food to cook. He was so helpful in with cutting up the strawberries. He asked me if I needed any help when he saw that I was having a little bit of trouble. I was more than happy to let him help me. Cutting things up was my least favorite thing to do in the kitchen. We both seemed to have our food done and in their respective places at the same time. It was so cute to watch him making his food. I always found it sexy to see a man cooking in the kitchen. The way he handled the noodles as he laid them in the lasagna pan was very delicate. He poured the sauce on the noodles with such precision that I couldn't help but be impressed. Currently he was at the stove making me his (apparently) famous apple cider.

"You see Sareya, you don't only drink apple cider during the fall. I have found that this is a delicious to drink to have anytime that it is cold."

"Is that so?"

"Oh, most definitely. I would just like to point out that it is indeed still January. In saying that you are also aware that it is still winter time. Correct?"

"You are absolutely right in that statement."

"Thank you for acknowledging. You see, I have been trying to tell my family this for years and they look at me like I'm crazy."

I giggled a little. "Well, I think that it's a logical statement. If it's cold outside I know I would want to drink something that was a hot beverage."

"See, that's the thing. For my family that's coffee. I personally don't like coffee that much so, I prefer to drink hot tea and apple cider."

"You don't like coffee either? Thank goodness! I thought I wasn't the only one on the planet that didn't drink it."

He turned back to me and gave me a look of what could only be explain as love.

"I am honored to say to you today that you are not the only one who doesn't like to drink coffee."

He gave me his beautiful smile this time as he turned back around to the stove. He was working very intently to make his special drink. I loved his focus and ability to multitask while he made it and carried on a conversation with me. I absolutely couldn't wait to taste it.

# 12
## CHAPTER

"MMMMM! I am excited to taste your lasagna Caius. It smells so delicious." I said. I set his lasagna on the pot holder that was on top the table. In a decorated ceramic bowl was the garlic bread that I had added in the last 10 minutes of our oven cooking time. It was the twisted bread kind that is my absolute favorite. Next to that I put the my beautifully decorated strawberry tart that has the strawberry open as if they are in bloom around the pie dish. Two candles were on the table and they were mock candles. The best part was you didn't have to set the candle on fire. Instead you simply flipped the switch and it would resemble a flame. They sat inside of a designed cylinder and reflected shapes around the kitchen. I preferred this over lighting a real candle. I learned over the years that I was bad about blowing them out when I was finished with them. Also located on the table I had two pairs of blue cloth napkins with a set of matching retro blue and white designed plates. Our glasses were made of crystal and had a nice swirl design to it. They were my favorite glasses. All of this was sitting on top of a soft yellow tablecloth. There was a dimmer for my great room and I had it set on low for our meal. You could without a doubt feel the ambience.

"This table setting is too wonderful for words. I don't want to eat anything on this table."

"Thanks. I feel the same how about we take a picture of it before we eat it all?"

"I love that idea. Matter of fact let me take it with my phone. This will be a first of many more wonderful dinners." I couldn't help but blush at his words. I hoped we had many more of them too. We positioned ourselves with our chairs next to each other and leaned in close to take our very first selfie. He counted down from three to let me know when to smile. I looked directly into the camera and reveled in the feeling of having him so close next to me. I could feel the warmth coming off him since he was so close to me. I looked directly into the camera lens as he put the camera in front of us and smiled just as he said the number three. He clicked the camera and we were forever placed in history on the SD card on his phone.

"Can we take another one? I want one more?"

Ok. That's fine."

"Can I put my arm around you this time and pull you closer to me?" I was too excited to hear him ask me that question.

"Sure. Go ahead."

"Ok."

He placed his arm around me and placed his face next to my cheek. It felt fabulous.

"Alright, are you ready?"

"Yep." He counted down once again from one to three and I made to make sure that I was looking directly into the lens of the camera. The last thing I wanted was to look like I was looking around or was bored in the picture. He announced three while I was looking into the lens and clicked the button. At the same time Caius snuck in a quick kiss on the cheek. I turned to look at him in surprise right after the flash went off. I was pleasantly surprised that he kissed me. What I sneaky way to get a kiss from me.

"Oh yea. I really like that one." He said with a look of pride on his face. He showed me the picture and somehow, he timed it perfectly. It only showed him kissing me and not me turning to look at him. I could not believe it. This man was crafty but, in a good way.

"It is a good picture." I happily admitted.

He was extremely satisfied at the fact that he snuck a kiss on my cheek. Trust me when I say he wasn't making any attempts to hide it from my gaze. He continued to look at me while I moved away from him. I put my chair back to the other side of the table. Caius decided to keep his chair where it was. He didn't move a muscle so, I made sure to place mine directly across from him.

"Why did you go all the way on the other side of the table? I got the impression that you liked being close to me."

"That's why I'm over here. I want to make sure there was some space between us." I admitted to him. I didn't feel that it was necessary to lie to him. Why would I start doing that now anyway? It was a little bit too late for that.

"That's ok then. As long as I get to see your lovely face I am truly content." Man, he was a smooth talker. I must make sure I don't fall for everything he says. Although, I somehow knew that I could believe everything that he said.

"Shall we pray over the meal?" I asked out of automatic response.

"Of Course." I didn't think there would be a problem after he quoted the scripture earlier. I figured anyone that knew that most likely prayed over his meals. I'm glad I made a good guess.

"Would you mind praying over the meal?"

"Sure." The prayer he gave for the meal was short and straight to the point. However, when he prayed you could tell that he was anointed by God with this gift. I knew immediately that I wouldn't mind hearing him pray over anything. Nothing said comfort to me more than a man that could pray.

When he finished the prayer we both reached for the spatula in the lasagna. We giggled, and I pulled my hand back to allow him to serve himself first.

"I apologize. I would love to be able to serve you."

"You would? Ok."

I laughed and asked me to bring up my plate. I did, and he placed a big portion of white lasagna on top. He then grabbed the tongs for the bread.

"Would you like some garlic bread?"

"Oh yes please!"

"Wow, you seem really excited about this garlic bread."

"That's because it's my favorite kind of garlic bread." I clapped as he placed my very own piece on my plate.

"You seem more excited about the bread more than my lasagna."

"Oh! Sorry, I'm happy about both. The presentation on my plate is gorgeous. Go ahead! Put it on your plate and see for yourself. I'm starving and ready to eat." He laughed as he went to serve himself.

"Ok, let's take our first bite together ok?"

"Ready? I'm about to go without you?"

"Alright, GO!" We both tasted the lasagna at the same time and it was delicious!

"MMMMMMMMMM!" I groaned in a very appreciative tone.

He wiped his mouth with his cloth napkin before he spoke. You could tell he was fully appreciating the flavors in his mouth as he finally swallowed his food.

"You got that right. It is good."

"Were you surprised? I know you made it?"

"Yea, I did but, I amazed myself."

I almost choked on my food. He was hilarious. I'm so glad we decided to do this dinner date at my house. It was obvious that he felt at home here and of course I felt at ease in my own home.

"Well, I love it when a man can cook. Not to mention I love to see a man physically in the kitchen cooking."

"You like that huh?"

"Oh, no. I love it." I admitted while I took another wonderful bite of his white lasagna.

"Well, I have only my dad to thank for that. He loved to cook, and he taught me how."

"He did huh?"

"Yep, I'll make sure to call him tomorrow when he gets off work."

"Hey, I would." I giggle

He's been such good company from the time that he got here. I was happy to learn that he was hilarious. Within 20 minutes we had finished the main entrée and were ready for dessert. He rubbed his hands in anticipation to the point where it made me nervous to serve it to him. I stood up to cut the tart with my cake serving spatula.

"Why are your hands shaking?"

"They're shaking because I'm nervous Caius."

"Why are you so nervous? It's only me."

I looked at him with my huge eyes. How could he not know the reason?

"That's exactly the reason why I am nervous. I want to make sure that you like it."

"I assure you that I am going to love whatever you make." He put his hands out with his plate in his hand. He was ready to taste it. I finally surrendered a piece of my strawberry tart. He placed his plate back on the table and dove right in with his fork. I took a piece, put it on my plate, and slowly sat down in my chair. I watched him like a hawk to see the reaction on his face as soon as it touched his palette. I was ecstatic to see that his facial expression was very pleased.

"Sareya…" "Kitten…." "This is the most mouthwatering dessert I have ever had. MMMM!"

"Yea!" I said in a childish tone. Dare I say I kicked my foot up in celebration. Ok. I did.

"Wow. This is so delectable. I love it." His eyes were closed as he spoke. It was as if he was imaging himself somewhere other than here.

"You look like you drifted off into another world"

"Mmmhmmm. A world full of you and these strawberry tarts. You have to make this for me again."

"I would love to. I enjoy baking a lot so, I wouldn't mind making you many different desserts."

"Do you enjoy cooking?"

"I definitely do. I find that mixing the food together is like a chemistry experiment. To see the outcome afterwards is totally amazing sometimes."

"I understand that feeling. I feel that way about baking. The only difference I find is that the presentation would be much prettier."

"Wait a minute. I feel that cooking gives the same results."

"I don't think so."

"I think it does. Some of the dishes I've made were have looked absolutely gorgeous in my opinion."

"Ok. Fine. Cooking can give off the same amount of beauty as baking does."

"I'm just saying. Some of the dishes that are made are presented in such a beautiful fashion that I don't even want to eat it."

"You are absolutely right about that. I am a true baking fan so, of course I'm going to say that baking looks more beautiful."

"I can't fault you for that at all." He raised his hands in surrender. I giggled to myself because I knew that he was picking on me a little bit. I liked it though.

"I'm thirsty now. You told me to drink water for my meal, right? Why did you ask me to that for again?"

He stood up in his seat and briskly walked over to the stove. He took out the mugs from my cabinets and poured the mixer into them. He walked over to the refrigerator, took out a can of whip cream, and walked back over to the stove. He removed the top from the top of the can and sprayed a lovely swirl of whip cream on top of the hot beverage. I watched him closely. His shoulders were pronounced through his shirt. I loved a man with broad shoulders and his looked wide and strong. His neck was strong as he turned around to carry the mugs back over to where I was sitting. My mug was placed in front of me and I noticed for the first time that he somehow quickly sprinkled cinnamon on top of the whip cream.

"Wow! Did you used to be a barista during high school?" I asked as I picked up my spoon to taste the drink.

"No. Thanks for noticing though." He laughed as he sat down with his mug.

"This presentation is beautiful Caius." I dipped my spoon into my mug and lifted out a mix of the hot beverage with the whipped cream. When I took my first sip I felt that I was in heaven.

"You like it huh?" I'm pretty sure he noticed that my eyes rolled into the back of my head.

"I love this apple cider. It is delicious. What is this extra flavor that I taste in here?"

"It is a caramel creamer."

My eyes lit up. "That is genius!" I said as I drank some more of the beverage even faster.

"Slow down kitten. There's plenty more if you want seconds."

I slowed down a little after realizing I was drinking it a bit too fast. It was delicious though. I couldn't think of the last time I have had anything this good before.

"Sorry, everything you have made has been like a fairy tale for me. I loved everything."

"You are very welcome. To tell you the truth you are the first woman I have ever cooked for."

"Really?"

"Yeah. You are very special to me. It was no doubt in my mind that you would enjoy a meal I made you. It was also a lot of fun cooking with you in your own home."

"I had a lot of fun too. I've never done this before either."

We both kind of blushed and look at our hands. Who knew it was possible. A short while later we finished our drinks. I stood to take the dishes to the sink after taking note that they were empty. We ate all our food. There was nothing left. There wouldn't be anyway. It was too good. He helped me take the dishes to the sink and rinse them, so they could be put in the dishwasher. We worked side by side again like we had been not too long ago. I was beginning to see how this would be in real life in the future. He put all the dishes into the dishwasher, put in a cleaning pod, set the dishwasher and closed the door.

"Thank you for helping clean up. You didn't have to do that"

"Your very welcome Kitten."

"Would you like to watch some TV?

"Sure."

I lead the way into the living room part of the great room. Grabbing the remote I turned on the tv and turned it to the food channel. The show Chopped was on so, I left it on. I loved most of the shows on that channel. We sat down together on the couch with me facing him. I wanted to make sure I could see his handsome face. I doubted he would mind me facing him anyway.

"Can I ask you a question?"

"I'll answer any question you want to know."

"Why do you call me kitten?" A facial expression full of delightment soared across his face.

"You've noticed did ya?"

"Yes. I did."

"I call you that because you remind me of a kitten. Whenever I touch you or hold your hand you close your eyes and lay your head to the side."

"I do?"

"Yep. You look so calm that if you could purr I know that you would."
I believed what he said. It was truly interesting to hear how it looked from
his point of view though. I nodded my head as I leaned along the back of
the couch.

"I like that pet name for me. You may keep it."

"Alright!" He said in triumph. "I'm glad you like your pet name for you."

"Did it just come to you?"

"Actually, Yes. You looked so content just like a cat. Then you're so
small that I could not help but think of you as a kitten." He softly grabbed
my right hand. He lifted it up to his mouth and kissed the back of my
hand. "Yea, just like that." I closed my eyes and laid my head on the back
of the couch.

"I can't argue when your saying I'm as cute as a kitten."

"I would hope not. You are just so adorable. How do you keep doing
this to me? You have no idea what you do to me do you?" He laughed.

"I'm sorry to say that I don't. I have absolutely no idea what I do to you."

"Well, let me enlighten you."

"You brought light into my life. I thought that being single and being
in my career was what I always wanted. I loved my life. Then I met you…."

I looked up into his eyes while he spoke to me. I wanted him to
know that I was paying attention. Man, he had such handsome face. Pay
attention to his face Sareya.

"You cracked the façade that I had created. It was helpless against you.
However, I am very happy that all my walls came tumbling down. You
are the most intelligent, beautiful, happy, career driven woman that I have
ever met. I am proud to say that you are my girlfriend. I love you Sareya."

# CHAPTER 13

His words washed over me like a clear blue wave on the beach of Jamaica. I felt happy. I felt complete. I felt scared. I just didn't quite understand. How could he love me? So soon. We just met. How did he know that he loved me already? I was flattered by the compliments that he gave me, and I couldn't help but wonder how long he had felt this way. I wanted to ask him when he first knew he felt so strongly about me. However, despite all these thoughts going through my mind I did feel strong feelings for Caius. Without any further reasoning I responded to his words in kind.

"Woah…" I said breathlessly. My eyes fell to look at the brown couch cushions. I grabbed the accent pillow that was behind my back. I placed it on my lap and looked back up into Caius deep brown eyes. He was waiting patiently. The sound of the TV was pronounced as he waited to hear my answer. A slow smile spread across my face as I the thought of him loving me staked a claim in my heart. The truth of the matter was…I loved him too.

"That makes me so happy to hear Caius. You have no idea." As soon as the words left my mouth I started to tear up. It was for the best. I wasn't ashamed to cry in front of him but rather I wanted him to know how important that meant to me.

"It does?" He asked. He slipped his arm around my shoulders and pulled me near him until we were side by side. He felt warm and without thinking I snuggled into his side.

"See, this is why I call you kitten. You are so adorable. Just stay there and don't move ok.?"

Looking up, I smiled. Even though I couldn't speak. At the same time, I knew he deserved to know how I felt.

"You are so precious to me Sareya. I want to be with you all the time. When I'm not I feel like a better part of me is missing. The funny thing is that I didn't even know that it was missing in the first place. I love you so much. My heart is overflowing right now from finally telling you how I feel. I can't get enough of you. I wanted you to know that."

"Thank you, Caius." I said with a shaky voice. Burrowing myself into his side I took a deep breath of his smell. It smelled like men's cologne and one of the many Axe soap line. I personally am a fan of the Axe line. It complimented his natural smell extremely well. Once again, this man knows how to dress.

"Come here." He said after letting me hide myself away for a couple about a minute. He reached down to gently cup my chin. He lifted my chin up aggressively and with a look of pure love he kissed me. His lips were so soft and reassuring. I wasn't afraid at all that he wanted me for sex. His kiss didn't say that to me at all even though it was aggressive. Instead I felt like he couldn't get enough of me. It was as if he didn't kiss me right now he would die. I liked this desperate kiss he was giving me. I put my arms around his neck to lift myself up a bit into his arms. With me being shorter I must make sure I'm high enough to be the most comfortable. In response to me lifting myself up he wrapped one arm me and with the other placed his hand on my cheek. A feeling of being captured was in full effect from this kiss. The best part was he hadn't French kissed me yet. If this was how we would be when we weren't French kissing I could only imagine what the feeling would be once we did. The sound of our breathing was audible over the TV and you could hear it start to become ragged. I knew what that meant. I slowly backed away from him to end the kiss but, he just moved me back closer to him. I giggled and gently pushed myself away from him. Trust me when I say I didn't want to move away from him.

He loosened his arms so that I could move away. Remained planted in his position on the couch I backed up back to where I was originally seated. Both of us watched the other as we let our breathing come back down to a calmer state. He looked disheveled a bit from me wrapping my arms around his neck. I guess I was doing more than I thought. Good thing I stopped myself in time. The look on Caius's face could only be described as sad that I pulled away. I know he understood why I did. I also knew that he didn't want to scare me. However, he also still had that look of desperation on his face. I wondered how I could help him be at ease after that.

"I love kissing you." I said with confidence.

"I do too. You have no idea." He said with a husky voice. Determined not to have the physical connection be broken for too long he held my held again. He must really be an affectionate man.

"I think I have some idea." I said assuredly. My chest was still raising itself up and down as I tried to lower my respirations. It wasn't easy to do with him right in front of me. Then unexpectantly he held my hand up to his left cheek. I held myself still as best I could while I watched him lean his face onto my hand. It was such a sweet gesture. I felt pretty and soft. To know that I put him at ease as much as he puts me at ease was a very pleasing sight to see.

"I made you feel at ease too huh?"

"Yes. You are honestly the only woman who has made me feel this way."

"Really? Wait a minute. How many girlfriends have you had?"

"Including you? Hmmmm 2."

"That's it?" I asked amazed at such a low number. How could he have only had two girlfriends in his life as handsome as he was.

"I didn't mess around with the girls like that. Many of them where I lived played too many games. I focused on school and sports instead."

"I can't fault you there. I didn't have that many boyfriends either for the same reason."

"Great minds think alike huh?" He said as he kissed the back of my hand.

"I guess so." He rolled my hand from his lips to his ear just softly rubbing it along his face. It felt really good.

"How many boyfriends have you had Sareya?"

"Three. None of them were serious though. At least not to them."

"What do you mean?"

"They all cheated on me. I used to think it was me but, then I realized it was just the type of men I was picking."

"I'm sorry to hear that. I don't know why any man would cheat on you."

"Well, it happened. When I asked them why none of them could give me a reason. I think it was because I wouldn't have sex with them, so they sought it out elsewhere."

"When was your last boyfriend?" Caius sat up all of sudden and gave me a serious looking. Or maybe he was thinking, I really couldn't tell.

"When I was 18. I was about to graduate from high school when he told me that he wanted to break up. He said that we just weren't on the same page. It's funny though. He never told me before that that he felt we were on separate pages. Back then I didn't know it was his way of doing the "it's not you it's me" thing. At the end of the breakup he finally admitted that he met someone else and they'd been dating for a while."

"What! That's bold!"

"Don't I know it. It was after that relationship that I decided to not date anymore and just have fun. I was going off to college. I was going to be staying on campus and I couldn't wait to experience new things. I just didn't realize that I would cause a huge problem for myself in the process."

Caius wrapped his arms around me really tight to the point where I almost couldn't breathe. Instinctually, I laid my head in the crook of his shoulder. I put my arms back around his shoulders and let him hold me. I could only imagine the thoughts that were going through his mind.

"I'm so sorry that happened to you Sareya. I really am sorry." He said as he rubbed my back. I could feel the anger and the pain he felt as he rubbed me. It had to have been hard for him to hear that this happened to me on three separate occasions. I don't fault him for what he was feeling. I know if the roles were reversed I would have angry and sad too.

"It was a long time ago so; you don't have to worry about it. I'm just glad that the Lord kept me in his hands and showed me the way out. In doing so he led me to you and I will forever be grateful for that."

"To think if I didn't agree to that the client to dinner I would never had met you." Shaking his head, he pushed me back so that he could see my face. He tenderly cupped my face in his hands and gently kissed me on the lips and then my forehead. I swear I could've just melted in his arms right then. He is so affectionate I loved it. I was always looking for a man who was affectionate and would be genuine about it. Caius was definitely a genuine affectionate man.

"I know. If my best friend hadn't gotten that job in town she wouldn't have ever came. If she never came I wouldn't have taken her to dinner so, I wouldn't have met you."

"Then I have to make sure I give your best friend an awesome gift." He laughed and leaned onto the back of the couch.

We laughed and talked for another hour or so and before we knew it 11:30pm was showing on the clock. It was a Saturday night so; it wasn't like we had to get up for work in the morning. I just wanted to make sure that he wasn't an early bird or anything. I am not by any means so, I could hang out into the wee hours of the night before I got tired. Besides I was with Caius. I was too excited to have him in my home to go to sleep anytime soon.

"Hey, remember how I asked you if you would like to go dancing with me?"

"Yes."

"Would you care to dance right now?" He asked. He stood up with an outstretched hand which signaled the universal ballroom sign for "Would you like to dance?"

"On my Pandora the easy listening was still playing, and a beautiful rumba began to play. Rumba was my favorite ballroom styles of dance so; I immediately took his hand. He walked me over to the space between the kitchen and the living and began to sway with me.

"Do you know how to do the Rumba by chance?" I asked as he swayed to the tempo.

"No, but I would love it if you could teach me." He said with a look of mischief in his eyes.

"Okay. Don't get any funny ideas ok? I will teach you." I showed him the basic step and how to glide his feet along the floor. After a couple of tries with my toes in danger of being smashed to death he was doing the basic move effortlessly.

"Am I doing it right?"

"Yep. You are actually a fast learner."

"Thanks. I've been told that with other things but, I'm glad it also applies dancing."

"I'm a fast learner too. I also love to learn new things. It's never a day you don't see me reading something."

"Is that right? What books do you like to read?"

"Some action, some drama, as well as romance. I like a good story that takes me to the location just from reading the pages. I admit I'm a sucker for romance novels though."

"Are you a hopeless romantic?" A teasing smile shot across his mouth. You could tell he was itching to tease me about this.

"Yea. I am. Knowing that God made love I have always been curious about the stories of how people met. I began to piece together certain aspects that led to them meeting, how they fell in love, and the length of time before they got married."

"You kept track of that."

"Well, not like a science experience just for knowledge. For example, I quickly noticed a pattern that most of the couples I spoke with normally had one person that really didn't like nor wanted to date that person they were currently married to in the beginning. If one was head over heels 9 times out of 10, the other person wasn't feeling them at all."

"That's fascinating. I can honestly say I never thought of that before."

"To be honest I don't think most people do. I tend to think outside the box most of the time. Growing up I always seemed to ask questions about things that nobody else cared about. I used to be teased for it but, when I got to college I learned that my way of thinking was very beneficial in my field of work."

"It sounds like you notice patterns very easily." He led me around the kitchen with ease. It was obvious that was already a good dancer.

"Pretty much. I'm a visual learner so, whatever you say I envision in my mind as your speaking to me. That in turn makes an image and after a while I notice a consistency. Working with computers and medical records have proved to have that really handy."

"I can imagine. I'm not a visual person myself. I'm a show me and I can do it type of person. Hence, you teaching me how to dance just now. I have found that working with computers requires that from time to time when it's not a standard program. I'll be the first one to ask how to do you do something. Telling me verbally doesn't always work for me either. It's best if you show me."

"I definitely can see that. Would you say always touching me goes hand and hand with that?"

"I would."

"Why is that?" The song we were dancing to ended. I felt kind of out of breath.

"I can feel your emotions when I touch you. When your happy or when you are sad your emotions flow from you to me in a simple touch. I can also feel it from you when I'm near you. I also noticed when I touch you that I that you like it. You never shy away from it. You never refuse my advances. Well, except when I tried to hug you during our first date. Other than that, you don't seem to mind me touching you. I can't help but see that it seems help you on an emotional level. Am I wrong?"

We were now standing in the great room having this conversation. Feeling that it was getting a little too deep for me I walked over to the kitchen to get something to drink. I had a can of Cherry Pepsi inside and took it out have a sip. I offered some to him as well, but he refused. He seemed more intent on what I was about to say. I figured it also made him feel anxious since I broke out connection again. To tell you the truth I felt the same way. I turned to face him again while I kept my ground at the fridge. I didn't want to come off as needy to him but, it was only right to tell him exactly what I was thinking. If I wanted this relationship to work, I would have to do just that. Tell the truth.

"Your absolutely right. Having someone touch me now the way that you do isn't scary for me. I don't' feel any other motives in your fingers nor do feel like you only want me for my body. The whole time that you have been here you've done nothing offensive. You have been a complete gentleman from arriving on time to dancing with me here my great room. You've look me in the eyes when you are talking to me. You hold my mind just because you want to touch me. You held me when I told you about how I cheated on and I could feel the pain from you when I was in your arms. You are just too good to be true. That is what truly scares me."

Caius looked alarmed. He opened his mouth to no doubt soothe me but, I held up my hand.

"Don't worry I'm not breaking up with you. Far from it." Relief rolled through his body at the sound of my words. I had no doubt in my mind that he was going to fight for me if he needed to. He would without a doubt try to encourage me to stay with me despite my doubts. "I have never had a man take me out to eat on a date before?" His mouth dropped. "I also have never had a man that I liked come into my house before. Lastly, I have never had a man cook me dinner before or cook dinner with me. These are all things that I have done for the first time and they have all been with you." I stopped to let my words resonate in his mind. His face continued to register surprise but, also if I wasn't mistaken joy. I set my can of pop down and walked over to him.

"Are you trying to keep your distance so that you don't scare me?" He nodded his head. "That's hard for you isn't it?" He nodded his head again.

When I was standing in front of me I held both of his hands in my own. He closed his eyes tight as if he was restraining himself. I opened his hands and placed them around my waist. His eyes opened and looked down into my own with a look of wonder. It was as if he was seeing me for the first time. He kissed the top of head again and held me close to him. I didn't stop him. I didn't want him to release me from his arms either. I wanted to stay there for the rest of my life if I could.

Another song came on the radio and we began to sway again. Instead of the Rumba we just rocked together moving in a circle. With his arms around my back he put his chin on the top of my head. In response I put my chest on his chest. His heart beat was beating steady under his thin sweater. It fluttered to the beat of its own drum. A drum beat that I wanted to play alongside with as well. He was so warm as we moved in unison together. I couldn't think of any other place I would have been than right here at this moment. After that song ended another one came one and we continued to move together in a circle. His right arm came up to rub my right cheek as we danced to the music. With each step I was falling more in love with this man. As much research as, I had done I never knew that love had layers. I was just beginning to get a taste of what it meant to finally fall in love with someone. The sad part was that as much as I loved this man, I just couldn't bring myself to tell him. At least right now. One day I would have to but, I didn't feel that it needed to be tonight.

# 14
## CHAPTER

The sun seemed brighter as I woke up the next day. It was Sunday and last night was the best night of my life. I had a wonderful 2nd date with a man that told me he loved me, and I loved him. He showed me in cooking together that he was a great team player. He also showed me that he was a great communicator. Ok, I know that these are qualities that a manager would look for in an employee but, in my defense, I am a manager of the HIM dept. at the hospital. There are things in my personal life that I want that are also qualities required in the workplace. Surely, I couldn't be faulted for that.

The sheets rustled as I moved underneath them to move to the side of the bed. They felt warm on my skin from sleeping so well during the night. When I got to the edge of the bed I pulled the duvet and the sheets back and set my feet on the floor. Surprisingly, the floor didn't feel cold to me this time. I looked down at my feet and saw that I had socks on. When did that happen? I reached over to my bedside table to grab my phone. On the screen it showed that I had a text message from Caius that was sent at 3:00 am last night. It was currently 10 am in the morning. Sliding the bar over I opened the phone and read the message.

"Hey Kitten, I had a great time with you last night. I just got home, and I wanted to let you know that I made it back safely. You are such a special woman and you have a great sense of humor. By the way, I wanted to know if you wanted to hang out with me today? Let me know when you wake up ok. I'm going to try and get to sleep. That will be hard to do since you're not with me. Love you. (Get used to it. Now that I've told you I'll be saying it a lot more often.)"

I walked into the bathroom while I finished reading his message. He was so detailed and sweet in his message that I was so happy that he wanted me.

"I wonder what he wants do to?" I thought when I got into the bathroom. I picked up my face towel and washed my fair. I noticed that I somehow remembered to remove my makeup and cleaned my face. Thankfully, since I did that last night I only needed to wash my face this morning and put on my facial lotion. I picked up my electric toothbrush to brush my teeth. It was the thing that I really enjoyed doing now that I had one. It made it a lot easier to make sure that I brushed my teeth properly. Once I was done at the bathroom sink I turned on my shower. Making my way into my walk-in closet I selected the outfit that I wanted to wear today. I didn't check the weather so; I went back into the bathroom to grab my phone. I had an app that showed me the weather on a day to day basis that was provided by the local tv station in the area. I opened it up and saw that today was going to be sunny with a high of 48. Man, I am so happy that I met this man in a mild winter.

I walked back into my walk-in closet and decided on a pair of faded skinny jeans and a thin sweater yellow sweater. My shoes would be a pair of cute black boots that come up to my calves. I love these boots. Laying them out on the chair in the closet I walked back into the bathroom to jump in the shower. It only took me five minutes in the shower and I was in the closet getting ready. Less than 10 minutes later I was dressed and ready for the day. I wanted to hurry up to contact Caius. I wanted him to know that I wanted to hang out as soon as possible.

Checking the time, it was now 11:00am. I picked my phone back up from the chair on the closet to dial Caius. I sat down in the chair and touched his name on my recent call log. The phone rang only once, and he immediately picked up.

"Good Morning." His voice was so sexy in the morning. It was the first time that I heard his voice early in the day so, I was taken aback for a moment. I didn't know what to say for a couple of seconds.

"Good Morning. How did you sleep last night?"

"I slept well after I drank some warm milk."

"You did not!" I laughed into the phone. I got up and walked into my bedroom.

"I wish I was lying to you. When I left your house last night at 2:30am I found it quite difficult to fall asleep. I believe I told you in the text message I sent you when I got home."

"Yea, you did. I'm sorry that you couldn't get to sleep."

"No, you're not. All women like to hear that a man was thinking about them before they went to sleep." I nodded my head.

"Ok, it did feel good to hear that you couldn't sleep well last night because you were thinking about me."

"See." I could hear him smile through the phone. I couldn't wait to see his face again.

"Just so you know; I thought about you too before I went to bed too."

"I believe you but, I don't think you had any trouble falling asleep though. You didn't respond to my text last night so, tells me that you fell asleep just fine." He said as if he was challenging me to lie to him. I giggled over the phone in response.

"See, I'm right again. Man, I'm two for two todays."

"Congratulations. Maybe that's enough for you to start your day huh?"

"Oh know. I could always have more. How about we go to breakfast? There's a place I've been wanting to take you to. Then if you're up to it we can go see a movie?"

"Sure. Sounds great to me. Where do you want to meet?"

"I was thinking I'd pick you up. Are you already up and ready?"

"I sure am." I said excitedly.

"Alright, that's what I'm talking about. I'll be there in 15 minutes okay?"

"Ok. I'll be waiting."

"I can't wait to see what you'll be wearing today. Oh yea! See you soon."

I hung up the phone while I ran to grab my purse. I forgot that he didn't live that far from me. Like always I am very organized make sure that I have my things together before he arrives. Since I have 15 minutes before he arrives I call Shania and Luann and put them in a conference phone call. They made me promise whenever I go on a date to let them know where I was going in case of an emergency.

"Good Morning again ladies! How are you two today?"

"Good Morning" They both say simultaneously.

"I was just calling to let you both know that Caius and I are going out on another date today."

"Wow, didn't you guys just have a date last night?" Luann asked.

"Sure did. He wanted to hang out today too. He wants to go to breakfast and then to see a movie after."

"Dang girl! That's what's up. I hope you have a great time. Hey, can you take a picture of both of you this time?"

"Yea, I'm in agreement with Shania. I want to see what he looks like."

"Ok. I can do that. I actually have been itching to take a picture of us too."

"Alright girl. You have fun. Don't do anything I wouldn't do. I am going back to sleep." Stated Shania.

"You were up late last night again huh Shania?" Asked Luann.

"You would know girl. You were out with me last night."

"Oh. You two went out last night huh? I'm sure you had a lot of fun."

"We did girl. We danced that night away. Not to mention Luann met someone last night while we were out."

"You did!" I exclaimed.

"Yea I did. He was ok. I wasn't really feeling him like that."

"Did you give him your number?" I inquired.

"Ha! No. He just hit on me at the club and I danced with him a little bit. That was it. When it was time to leave I didn't give him my number."

"It felt good getting hit on though wasn't it?" Shania asked.

"It did. I'm not going to lie. No. He just hit on me at the club and I danced with him a little bit. That was it. When it was time to leave I didn't give him my number."

"It felt good getting hit on though wasn't it?" Shania asked.

"It did. I'm not going to lie. No. He just hit on me at the club and I danced with him a little bit. That was it. When it was time to leave I didn't give him my number."

"It felt good getting hit on though wasn't it?" Shania asked.

"It did. I'm not going to lie about that." She laughed.

I walked into the great room with my things to make sure I was ready for Caius when he got there. I set my things down on the couch and looked at the clock on the wall to see what time it was. I literally had 2 minutes left before he would be arriving so, I needed to cut this conversation short. I jumped back in right as Shania teased Luann about the way she dances.

"I know Luann is not the best dancer but, ladies I have to go. He will be here any minute so, I gotta go."

"Alrighty then. We'll talk to you later." Luann said.

"Yea, have fun and don't forget to send us a picture of you two."

"I will. Talk to you two later. Bye"

"Bye" They both replied. I hung up the phone and checked myself out one last time. I had a mirror on the wall in the living room so, I was able to check my whole outfit. I looked good. I walked over to the window that faced the front yard. I looked out the window to see him pull up. I felt like a kid waiting for the ice cream truck to arrive on my street. I was too excited for him to get here. It was only moments later when I saw him pull up heading my way. He rolled up into my driveway and parked his SUV. I hurried up to grab my purse and put on my jacket. I walked outside and locked my front door before he could even make his way to my front door.

"Hey beautiful! Can I pick you up?" He said. He was wearing an orange sweater with a pair of blue jeans with black boots. Kangoo must have been his favorite line of hats because he had one on that covered the shape of his head. It looked nice on him.

I turned to him and jumped into his arms. "I missed you." I said into his shoulder.

"I missed you too kitten." He said as he lowered me down to the ground. He held me close as he looked into my eyes. I got on my tiptoes so that I could do what I'd wanted to do since I woke up this morning. I kissed him. His lips felt warm and they were so moisturized. I pulled away after a little bit and jumped up and down in his arms from pure happiness.

"I'm so happy to see you too. I was going to ask you if I could kiss you but, I am very happy to see that you were thinking the same thing." He commented excitedly.

"Yes, I was." I smiled so hard you could see all of my teeth.

"Are you ready to go then?"

"Mmhmm. Let's go."

About 10 minutes later we were sitting in IHOP which is my favorite breakfast place to go to eat. I ordered my favorite which was the New York

Cheesecake Pancakes with turkey bacon and scrambled eggs. He ordered an omelet that he customized himself along with scrambled eggs and turkey eggs. To drink we both ordered orange juice but, he also asked for tea. As the waiter walked away I took a sip of my orange juice.

"Why did you get the turkey bacon?" He asked.

"I was raised in the Seventh-day Adventist Church and the church specialized in the health message written in the bible. I wasn't raised to eat certain foods because they are on that list of animals that are not good for you to eat. When I got older I did research for myself and learned that the list did have animals/bugs that were bad for you. Pork is on that list. Just to name two things they are high in fatty acids and they eat everything which makes them bottom feeders. I'm sorry but, I don't want to eat anything that eats everything it can get its hands on."

"I understand that. I figured the reason you got turkey bacon was for that reason. I've never had turkey bacon so I'm going to give it a try."

"It's delicious. You should like it."

"I'm sure I will. Are there other animals on that list that you don't eat?"

"Yea. I don't eat seafood like crab or lobster."

"What! How can you live without eating lobster?"

"Well, for the same reason I don't eat pork. They're high in salt and are bottom feeders as well. I did try it when I got older but, I didn't like it."

"Well, since you tried it I can let it go then." He laughed as he sipped his hot tea.

"Oh yea. Just like most people I wanted to try what I couldn't have growing up. However, after learning for myself why those animals were put on that list I decided to not eat those foods. I also saw growing up that those who stuck to this list were healthier and lived to be old. That also helped me make my decision as an adult."

"I can understand that. Your family must be really healthy then?"

"Mhmm. No one in my immediate family has diabetes, high blood pressure, heart disease, aren't overweight etc."

"That's amazing. I wish I was told about that growing up. I don't feel that eating the food on that list from time to time is bad though."

Just then our food arrived. The waiter placed our plates in front of us and I couldn't wait to take a bite of my food. We both bowed are heads to pray over our food and then we commenced with our conversation.

"I understand what you're saying. I don't have any of those foods in my house though so, that's something I'm not willing to negotiate with."

"Man, you just went straight to that huh?" He laughed as he took a bite of his omelet.

"Well, I think it's important you know that upfront. Wouldn't hate to hear that after we get deeper into the relationship? If I were a vegetarian it would be important for me to say up front isn't it?"

"Your right about that. Thanks for telling me. I would like to try your diet. The results that you've spoken of sound good. Surely it couldn't be that bad to give up pork and seafood."

"I'm not saying that you have to do that. I just wanted to let you know since you asked me. Please don't feel pressured to change your diet."

"Actually, I value my health so to hear this from you I am willing to give it a try. I want to see what differences I will see." I smiled and cut into my cherry cheesecake. When I took a bite, it was so tasty. It'd been awhile since I had been here. I was so happy to have this breakfast again.

"You like those pancakes huh?"

"Hmmm...?"

"I can tell. Your eyes rolled into the back of your head."

"Oh." I giggled.

"May I have a bite?"

"Sure. I turned my plate, so he could cut a piece of my pancakes from the side I hadn't eaten from yet. He placed the pancake in his mouth and within seconds I heard the familiar sound of approval coming from his mouth.

"MMMMMM. This is delicious."

"I know right." I said as I took another bite.

"You said you were raised Seventh-Day Adventist, right?"

"Yes. What were you raised as?"

"Pentecostal." I nodded my head to let him know I was familiar with it since my mouth was full a food.

"My siblings and I grew up in the church and were involved in just about everything you could think of." He laughed.

"Ah. Your parents had you all do everything huh?"

"Pretty much. My family is musically inclined so, they made sure all of us learned an instrument."

"You can play an instrument?"

"Yes. My voice."

"Ooooh, I love a man that can sing."

"Do you now?" He looked up at me with a seductive look.

"Oh yea!" I nodded my head very slowly to emphasize my point.

"Would you like to hear me sing?" I nodded my head fast to emphasize my point. I am a dramatic person.

"How about I sing to you when I drop you off later tonight? Does that sound good to you?"

I dropped my fork on the plate in a retort. I did not want to wait till the end of the day to hear my new boyfriend sing. Do I really have to wait?

"Why? Can't you do it when we get back in the car?"

The laugh he gave me was so genuine. He even clapped in tandem with his laugh. It made my heart warm up to hear it coming from his mouth. His teeth were so white and perfect as he laughed. I don't think that I'll ever get sick of seeing it.

"How can I say no to such a beautiful face."

"Exactly. How could you say no. Please sing in the car? Please! Please!"

He turned his head to the side and took a good look at me. You could tell that he was very amused. He turned his head to the side and took a good look at me. You could tell that he was very amused. I wanted him to be. If he liked what he saw, I thought that maybe he would do what I asked of him.

"Ok. I'll send for you in the car."

"Yea!!!!!" I exclaimed in victory.

"I'm glad I can make my baby smile."

"Hmm? You just called me baby. Why did you call me that?"

"You are precious to me. It's the name I call you when I talk to my family and friends about you."

"You've been talking about me with your family huh?"

"Yea, I couldn't wait to tell my best friend about you. He is very happy that I have found someone like you. He was beginning to not believe in love himself."

"Why is that?"

"Well, he's older by 8 years and he has had trouble in his dating relationships. Due to them not working out he had begun to doubt that true love even existed. When I told him that I found someone he was too thrilled for me. Matter of fact he can't wait to meet you."

"I told my friends about you too. Oh, they wanted us to take a picture so, I can finally show them what you look like."

"Ok. Let's take one right now."

He moved over from his seat to mine then scooted in close while I got my camera ready. As soon as we were in position I pushed the button. Within moments we had taken our 2$^{nd}$ picture as a couple. This time it was forever documented in history on my phone. We both looked at the picture. It looked so pretty. We looked so happy and perfect in a way. I had to print it so that I could place it in a picture frame on my desk. I put my phone back in my purse then turned to see that Caius was still sitting next to me. We had finished our meals by this point so, we really didn't have to sit apart. I just didn't expect him to stay here I guess.

"Are you going to go back to your seat?" I inquired.

"I think my seat is right here. Don't you think?" I turned my face away as I blushed from ear to ear. He put his hand under my chin and turned my face so that I was facing him again.

"Don't look away kitten. I love to look at your reactions. Especially when I'm the one that's causing them."

"You're really not helping me right now Caius."

"I want to make you happy. If you reflect the love that I'm giving to you I want to see it." He said as he softly rubbed my chin. He looked down into my eyes while placing his other hand on my cheek. I didn't care if anyone saw us kiss in the restaurant. I've always like public displays of affection. It let people know that I had someone that truly loved and cared for me. It also showed others that he was proud to say that I was with him. For him to also like PDA made me so happy it practically made my day. He leaned in and rubbed our noses together. It was such a small gesture but so mighty at the same time. He then kissed my kissed chastely. Like always the electric current went coursing through my veins. Lastly, he kissed my forehead. What he basically showed me was exactly what he had already told me. I love you, your precious to me, and I will always cherish you. How I had longed for this triple combo. Today it is finally mine and no sex was involved in it whatsoever.

"Thank you." I said as we looked at each other again.

"For what?" He asked as he absentmindedly rubbed his thumb along my cheek.

"For showing everyone that I'm yours. It feels good to be marked. There was a time that I thought that this would never happen."

"You did?" I lowered my head thinking back to the men I'd met in my life. None of them wanted to be exclusive. They all wanted to just "Kick it" as they would say, and I thought that was the only way to get a man. I didn't know at the time that I was sadly mistaken.

"Yea." I said as I continued to look down. Why did I still feel ashamed of what happened back then. He always told me that he didn't care so, why was I still fixated on this. I needed to let it go. I didn't want to have this be an issue in our relationship. I wanted to start fresh with this gorgeous man in front of me.

"Sareya, I am proud to say that you are my girlfriend and I am even more proud to say that you are a fighter. You made it through that time of your life with God leading the way. That shows me that you're not a force to be reckoned with. I am blessed to have you by my side."

I slowly lifted my head to look into his eyes. He was looking so sincere that there was no way that he was lying to me. He held my hands gently in his own. I lifted them up so that I could rub my face on his hands. The same hands that make me feel special. The same hands that make me happy. The same hands that make me feel wanted all from their gentle touch. These hands were my man's hands.

"Awwww. You are just too cute. Come here." With that he lifted my head so that he could kiss me again.

# 15
## CHAPTER

The restaurant was buzzing with excitement this bright Sunday morning. The weather was pretty much feeling like spring. Happily, I able to now say, with Caius in my life I was too. I stared at him as I drank my hot chocolate. His face was so beautiful. His skin was so smooth. His small eyes were in a state of remembrance as he recounted a story to me about his siblings. It was very funny hearing his stories as a child. However, I couldn't get past that fact that I wanted to touch his face. It was quite difficult but, I feared that I did that I would possibly go too far. I wanted to just enjoy this moment and relish in it for as long as I could. For the time being I was content to just stare at him from across the table while he drank his tea. When he opened his mouth, he spoke intelligently and confidently. His words were strong. His words were also soothing. This form of intimacy was what I had always wanted. Conversation could be very intimate. I had read about it so many times in my romance novels that I was convinced that it existed. It had to. At this point how could I not. Sitting before me right now was intimacy incarnate. How could a man give me such a sense of conviction the way that he did? I don't know but, I was beginning to like it.

Before I know it it's time to leave the restaurant. I was feeling good. It was a great breakfast as to be expected with Caius. I was coming to realize that this man had to be the one. To be honest I had never felt this way about anyone before. I had wanted to feel that way with my ex's before but, they never turned out to be the "one". Looking back, I saw emotionally just how desperate I was to find true love. I was willing to lower my standards at the time to make a man happy. This lesson I had learned a couple years ago. From then on, I resolved to never settle again. I also asked God to let me know when I met my husband. I didn't want to waste anytime dating a man that wasn't meant for me. At this point I hadn't heard anything but, I felt that he was meant for me. Our waiter brought our check soon after. I started to gather my things so that I would be ready to head back out to the car. We stood together, and Caius reached for my hand.

"I miss your touch." He said simply. He looked so honest with his response. Although, he was technically right. We were too close to hold hands so, he had his arms around my shoulders. He held me tight for a long time at the restaurant. He was so sweet and gentle. I held out my hand and took a hold of his. We walked together to the cashier hand in hand. This was the way that I preferred to do it. Another symbol of public display of affection. A declaration of "I'm his everyone. Don't touch." This statement was extremely important to me. While I waited for him to pay I laid my head on his right shoulder. This didn't prove to be a challenge for him since I saw him use his left hand to retrieve his wallet. This man was ambidextrous.

He held the doors open for me as we walked back out to the car. The weather was still sunny with a high of 45 degrees. With only my jacket on I was nice and warm. After he opened the car door for me to get in I took it off. The interior of the car was too warm to keep it on. It just wasn't necessary.

"Awwww." I said as I exhaled a deep breath.

"What was that sound for?" He asked at the same time he started the car. He turned to me to caress my cheek once more.

"Nothing. I'm just very happy." I smiled. I turned my head toward him so could see the look on my face.

"I'm happy to hear that. It makes me happy to know that you are happy." He smiled back at me. He then turned to face the front of the car. "Shall we do a movie. Or are you too full?" He asked smoothly.

"I'm up for a movie."

"Alright. There's a musical that's out that I think you are going to love." He said as he backed out of the parking lot.

Caius was a good driver. I was satisfied with watching him as he drove. I decided to do it again. Suddenly, I heard I saw a bright light shone around Caius. It was a beautiful golden light that was surrounding him. It encased him but, he didn't notice the light at all. It was as if I could only I could see it. He continued to drive to the theatre as if nothing was happening. I studied the light closely and saw little fractals of what I could only describe as glitter floating down through the light. Then I heard a voice speak to me.

"This man is your husband."

"What!" I thought. This man? Tears started to burn in my eyes as the realization set in. This was the Lord speaking to me. I knew that. I had heard his voice before. He said it to me as if he was sitting right next to me in the car at this very moment. He responded to my doubt quickly.

"Sareya, he is your husband." Instantly I saw images of the man that Caius was going to become. A strong Christian man that helped people and would be a witness for the Lord in everything that he did. I saw how he would look when he got older as well. It was an awesome sight to behold. God showed me how we would be working together in his name. This was truly a vision that God was giving me.

Smiling and with my eyes closed, I conveyed my thanks to him mentally. "Thank you, Father, for this man. I remember asking you to let me know when I met my husband during my deliverance. Thank you for telling me that he is the man you made for me. Help me to be the woman you called me to be in your name as well. Thank you. Thank you. Thank you. I love you Lord."

When I opened my eyes, the light began to slowly fade away. Tears ran down my face as a reaction to the revelation I just witnessed. The feeling of joy was filling me up to the point that I couldn't hold contain it. I also sit still now. Instead, I leaned over and kissed Caius on the cheek. He looked at me momentarily and smiled at me. This intimacy. This romance. It was just beginning.

The movie was so much fun with Caius. I learned that he likes musicals too. He knew some of the songs in the movie and I got to hear his voice for the first time. He sounded wonderful. Just like his speaking voice he was confident as he sang. He was also very animated just like me. We talked about our favorite scenes conversely in tandem. There was no predilection in our conversations. It was open and free to express yourself without judgement. I was enjoying every moment of it.

"I'm craving some ice cream."

"MMM, that does sound good."

"If you would like there is a place not too far from here that has some of the best ice cream around?"

"Sure." I giggled. "Can we walk from here?"

"Yep. It's this way."

That was the benefits of living in a big city. All your conveniences were close by. I left my hometown for that very reason. It wasn't that it was small but, in comparison I went from 24.42 sq. mi to 368.1 sq. miles. It is consequently much bigger.

"I think it's just a couple more blocks and then we'll be there."

"Ok. That's fine with me. I'm enjoying my time with you. I don't want it to end."

"I'm having a great time too. I don't want it to end either."

Walking hand in hand down the city streets felt perfect. We passed many shops along the way that were small business owned. That's one thing I loved about this city. They supported small businesses. When we walked past one on the way to the ice cream shop it had an alluring outfit on a mannequin in the store window. I stopped to look at it closely intrigued by the beading and the gracefulness of the skirt flowing down from the back of the mannequin. The top of it was cut in a V shape neckline and the dress was sleeveless. It made to be form fitting to accentuate the girls of the woman wearing the dress. In its breathtaking red color, I felt enriched with a sense of importance just looking at it. Coming to step behind me Caius eyed the dress that I was seriously craving to have for myself.

"It's beautiful isn't it." He said suggestively.

"Yes, it is." I whispered. I wondered how much it was?

"Do you want to go inside and get a closer look? He had a boyish grin on his face as he led me to the store's front door.

"Is it still open?" He looked at the hours on the door.

"He sure is. It's only 5pm and they're open until 8pm." In the next movement he held the door open for me then gently pushed me through the door.

Once inside I could smell the fresh new clothes smell. It was a distinct smell that I remembered from childhood. It made me think of my mother whenever I smelled it. It wasn't like my mom shopped a lot. On the contrary, it was my father who does all the shopping but, for some reason whenever I thought about new clothes or shoes I always thought of my mother. The floor was made of concrete as well as the walls. It gave it an industrial feel very similar to the deli Shania and I had visited earlier. The had an assortment of clothes from shirts, to pants, to dresses lined up. From what the tags told me the sizes ranged from X-small to X-Large. They were having a sale and the clothes were 30%-60% off. I was walking over to the mannequin in the window when a sales associate greeted us. She was very professional despite the age she portrayed to be. Her hair was black, short, and had her hair in a ponytail. She looked to be in her teens but, when she spoke she had to have been older. She asked if we needed any help with anything. Caius spoke to her for because I was so focused on looking at the dress that I didn't respond to her question.

"Oh Yes, that dress is very pretty. Let me check for you. I think it is also on sale. I'll be right back." She said excitedly. While we waited for her to return Caius stood next to me and put his arm around my waist.

"I think this dress would look phenomenal on you kitten." He kissed the side of my forehead softly to help emphasize his words. It did the job.

I turned to look at him. "Do you? I don't think it would look good on my body type."

"Hmmm." He put his hand on chin then took a step back to look at me real hard. "I think you have the perfect body type for it."

The way he indulged me was just ridiculous. He made me feel so beautiful it was just absurd but, in a good way. I couldn't help but feel cherished.

"You are in luck! That dress is on sale for 60% off its regular price. That makes it on sale now for 48.00." The sales associate said.

"Wait a minute! This dress was $120.00?" I exclaimed with a shock expression on my face.

"It sure was. You came in at a good time. We're starting to get rid of our winter line to get ready for our spring line of clothes. Although, in my opinion this dress could be worn in the fall or cool summer nights too. The material is breathable so, it allows you to wear it all round. It's an excellent purchase I guarantee you."

I looked at the dress again and saw what the sales associate said wasn't wrong. It could be worn all year round.

"Would you like to try it on babe?" I noticed that he asked me with his public pet name for me. He doesn't want anyone to know my other pet name. That was exclusively just for him.

"Yes. I do."

"Wonderful!" The sales associate proclaimed. I will go and retrieve the dress for you in your size. The dressing rooms are located at the very back of the store. If you head, there ahead of me I will be more than happy to bring the dress to you." This one of the reasons why I loved small businesses. The personal attention you get is like none other. They truly value your patronage and treat you like they would want to be treated. It's a basic bible principle but, many don't follow it. If you want people to treat you right, you must treat them right too.

"Thanks." I walked with Caius to the back of the store toward the fitting rooms. We passed racks after racks of other clothing but, I didn't think twice about stopping to look at them. All I had my mind set on was trying this dress on. They were located at the back of the store in a hallway that spiraled around. Caius decided to wait outside. He wanted me to walk out and show him how the dress looked once I had it on. I didn't mind doing that for him. When you got back there it opened into a room with various colored purple striped wall papered walls and the same concrete floor. There was cute accent black area rug located in the center of the room which was shaped in a big square. There was a total of 8 doors to choose from and they were all painted black. The doors were open just waiting to be used. I found this to be quite helpful where in other stores you must wait for the sales employee to come and unlock it for you. I have gotten myself locked out of the changing room because of this.

"Alright. Here you go. Go ahead and try it on. I'll be waiting right here when you are ready. She told me.

"I walked into the first changing room on my right and shut the door. There was a body length mirror on the inner wall that had a golden border that went around it. It looked very classy in my opinion. The walls were painted white and there were hooks strategically placed on the door and the walls. They made sure to give you adequate hooks to hang your coat and your clothes. There was also a long bench on the left side of the changing room. I was very happy to see that it was in this room. I have been to some where there was no bench but, they did give you a chair. This proved problematic in the winter when you had a big coat, your purse, and a bundle of clothes that you were looking to try on. I hung the dress up on the hook that was found on the back of the door. I then proceeded to undress myself. This never took me a long time. In a matter of minutes. I had my clothes off and the dress I wanted so badly on me.

When I slid it over my head the fabric was extremely smooth texture to it. It felt like it was wrapping me silk from what I could tell. I knew it wasn't made of silk though. It was made of something else and whatever it was it felt wonderful. The dress had no zippers or buttons to it so, I didn't need to worry about that fact. I liked dresses like this. It made it easy to put them on and to take them when you're a single woman. This was something I didn't understand would become an issue until I moved out on my own after college.

"How is it coming in there?"

"I'm ok."

"Do you like it?"

"I don't know. I haven't look at it." I'm pretty sure the young woman could sense my hesitation.

"Come on out and let me look." Yep, she did. I opened the door and stepped out of the dressing room. I let the door close behind me and waited to hear the harsh critique I was about to receive.

"You look great. How does it feel on you?"

"I love the way it feels."

She checked to make sure nothing was loose on me. It must have been satisfactory because, she was smiling hard.

"Why don't you talk it out so, your boyfriend can see."

"Do you think I should?" I asked timidly.

"Oh Yea. Trust me. He's going to love it on you."

Her words sunk in for a moment before I began to focus on the man waiting for me outside the changing room. He's the man God just told me is for me so, why am I sitting her contemplating if he'll like what he sees or not? I took a deep breath and walked back out to where Caius was sitting. When I came out he was looking at his phone no doubt playing a game of some sort. However, when I had made it into his line of sight his head shot up. He took a good look at me with the dress on for a long time before he spoke. The look on his face looked like he wanted to ravish me right here and now. I froze in place so that he could examine me very closely. My eyes were steadfast on him. I couldn't look anywhere else but, at him.

He stood up and slowly made his way over to me. He walked around me while skimming me from head to toe. I felt like an investigation was taking place now. He'd seen me in a dress before but, this was on different level. When he made his way to be standing in front of me again his eyes were full of passion. It made me look down from the power coming from behind his eyes. He wouldn't let me look down though. He lifted my chin back up and made me hold my gaze.

"Why are you looking down?" He said in an authoritative tone. I couldn't answer him. The way he spoke to me made excited. I had to back-track for a moment and remembered who I was now. I didn't want to get caught up like I had been before. He asked me the question again.

"Why are you looking down Sareya? Tell me the truth." He said while searching my eyes.

"I looked down because you look like you want to ravish me any second now. It made me kind of excited." His eyes grew huge for a moment. He removed his hand from my chin and placed it on my cheek. Suddenly, his mood shifted slightly to the look of love he was giving me earlier. It was as if I reminded of something.

"I'm sorry. I didn't mean to make you uncomfortable." The searing heat that I had just felt for the first time coming from him was now gone. I missed it. I wanted to feel it again but, I didn't know if I'd be able to hold back before we would go too far. I wanted him to touch me though. Show me the affection that he does every moment that he's with me. However, this time he made sure not to touch me while he was in that kind of mood.

"It's ok. I see that you like the dress?"

"Yes, I most certainly do. We'll have to find a place for you to wear this."

"What I didn't say that I was going buy it yet."

"Really? It looked like that to me when you were drooling all over it looking at it through the store window a little bit ago." He laughed. I couldn't be mad at what he said. He was right.

"That's true. It feels incredible on me."

"And it looks incredible on you. Let's get it."

"Ok."

"Great. I'll be waiting out here for you once your changed ok."

"Ok."

He leaned down and kissed me. It was urgent yet soft at the same time. I could feel the love and the urge was feeling for me all at the same time. It was incredible. I had never felt anything like this before.

"Go now before I regret what I do next." He turned me around and I walked back into the changing room. The young sales associate was in the hallway when I got back.

"It would seem that he likes it. The question left to ask would if you liked it?"

"I do very much. I'll take it."

"Wonderful. I'll go to the register to ring it up and I'll just wait for you there ok?"

"Thank you. That'll be just fine."

I took off the dress and handed it back to her to ring up while I got redressed. Before I knew it, I was at the register about to pay for my new dress.

"Alright, your total comes to 58.75. Will that be cash, check, or card?

Before I could take out my wallet Caius was already handing the woman his card.

"Wait a minute. You're paying for my dress?

"Nope, I'm buying it for as a first-time gift from me to you. You wanted it so bad that I couldn't not getting it for you. I want to give you more things and spoil you." He put his forehead on mine. "Get used to it." He smiled and took his card back from the sales associate.

"I can honestly say I am surprised."

"Why is that?" He asked with a boyish grin on his face. "Is it not right of me to want to spoil you?"

He took the bag for me and thanked the store for their help. I was still in shock over the facts from the last hour. It was all too much too fast. How could I explain this feeling to him without freaking him out?

"I have never had a boyfriend buy me anything before." There I think that was simple enough.

"Really? Not even a stuffed bear or chocolate candies?"

I shook my head. Caius did not look happy about that at all.

He opened the door for me with a look of anger. He had that same look when I told him that I had never gone out on a date with a guy before. He didn't say anything for the rest of the walk to the ice cream shop.

# 16
## CHAPTER

We held hands as we made our way to the ice cream shop that was now only one block away and stepped inside. New smells of vanilla, chocolate, and waffle cones filled the air from the second you stepped through the door. I felt quite giddy. This day was turning out to be just like the one I had imagined for the longest time up until this point anyway. Caius wasn't very happy with the latest news I gave him about never receiving gifts from a boyfriend before. I didn't try to speak to him since we were still walking to the ice cream shop holding hands so, I didn't think that I needed to say anything. I figured he was just processing the information thoroughly. He worked in cyber security after all.

We walked up to the counter to order our desserts. We had eaten at the theatre since they had a restaurant located within the building so, now I just wanted dessert. I ordered the hot fudge sundae covered in peanuts. That was my favorite ice cream style dessert to get aside from milkshakes. Caius ordered a medium size turtle sundae for his dessert. Walking down to the other end of the counter we picked up our ice cream and he paid for our food. This was a date after all but, now I was beginning to become conscious about how much he was spending on me. It wasn't like I was thinking that he shouldn't spend on me for date stuff but, now that he was spending money on things like dresses and stuff I was beginning to get uncomfortable.

"What's that look for? What are you thinking about?" He was cautiously. I could tell that he was concerned most likely because of the look on my face. The truth was I was also still worried the look on his from a few minutes ago.

"I was wondering why you looked angry when we left the store."

I let that hang in the air for a couple of seconds. He looked surprised or maybe more so upset at himself that I had noticed his reaction. We sat at a nearby table sitting side by side. I could tell that he wanted to protect me in way but, I wasn't quite sure why. Shaking his head, he put his spoon down and put his hands in his lap. He then to a moment to close his eyes to gather his thoughts.

"Sareya, everything your telling me in the truth correct."

"Yes." I replied. I set my spoon down and set up straight to make sure I gave him my undivided attention.

"You didn't have many boyfriends right."

"No."

"What did you do with them? If they didn't' buy anything or take you out on dates what did, they do?"

"We hung out at their house."

"Did any of the guys you dated have jobs or any money?" I could see where this was going.

"One did."

"I see. What was the reason the guy gave you for not buying you anything or taking you out on a date?" He's not going to like this answer at all.

"He said he needed all the money he had to give to his mother to help pay for the bills."

He looked upset.

"You mean to tell me that he couldn't spare some money to even buy you some candy on Valentine's day?" I hung my head in shame. I didn't know back then that the guys were only using me for sex. I thought if I gave them what they wanted that they would fall in love with me. That in turn would make them want to buy me things but, that never happened. I was tossed aside as soon as they were bored with me. That vicious cycle continued for 4 years.

"No, don't lower your head. You are not to blame for them using you like that." He said assurantly. I began to tear up at his words. It hurt so bad to admit this to him. I was relieved to know that he still didn't think ill will of me. He still loved me despite my stupid mistakes. Despite that though, it still wasn't easy to admit at all.

"They strung you along and that's all there is to it. I want you for you. Not your body. Don't get me wrong, I love the way you look. You are the sexiest woman I have ever seen in my life. Not to mention your smart, funny, Christian, and fun to be around. That's a hard diamond to find in a thick of coal that surrounds you every day. Somehow, I found you and you are spectacular."

He pulled me into an embrace and held me there for a couple of minutes. He didn't ask if he could but, I didn't care. I was crying and shaking so bad that it felt good to finally let all of this out. One by one my tears fell onto his shoulder until I finally stopped shaking. Once I had stopped moved away from me and smiled.

"You are mine now. No one will ever hurt you again. Ok?" He said while holding my face in his hands.

"Yes, I understand."

Driving home from the ice cream shop was simply being in bliss. It looked like it was 12:00 am when it was only 7:00 pm. The light posts shined brightly in the night when we drove past them. I always found them magical in a way at night time. When I was a child I used to dance around them for fun. Oh, to be child again. I wouldn't have made nearly as many mistakes that I had made.

"Would you mind if I came over this evening? I know we both have work in the morning but, I just can seem to be able to tear away from you right now. Can we just prolong it a little longer?"

"I don't see why not. It's not like I go to sleep before 11pm anyway."

"Good." I was happy that he was excited about coming over. It wasn't long before we pulled into my driveway and we were walking inside of my house together. It felt so good. It felt so right.

"Make yourself at home. I tell him. He stands at the door staring at me. "What's wrong?" Without a word he walks over to where I was standing in the great room, grabs me, and gives me our first French kiss. I kiss him back enthusiastically. My mind wasn't filled with shame and my mind wasn't filled with regret. All I could think about was Caius and how good it felt to be in his arms. We stayed like that for who knows how long until he picked me up off the floor. In that swift movement I dropped my jacket along with my purse.

"I'll get them later." I thought as he walked me toward the nearest wall. I couldn't believe what happening. Caius was kissing me in my house. Right now! It felt good. It felt so right but, then I remembered what my kryptonite was. Body Contact. I pulled away from him straight away making sure that I wasn't touching him at all. He blinked his eyes twice before he registered what had just happened. I could tell in the next moment that he felt bad for what he had done.

"I'm sorry Sareya but, I want you so bad. I apologize. Maybe I should go." He looked very disappointed in himself. I didn't want him to feel that way. I stopped him so, I knew that it was ok, and I didn't want him to leave. We are human after all. It would be unwise to assume that we wouldn't desire each other at this point. The hard part for me was making sure this all happened in the correct order.

"It's fine Caius. Really. I don't mind kissing at all. I'm ok with that. It's being so close body to body that I can't handle. It's better if we don't kiss that way. Other than that, I'm ok."

He let out a big sigh of relief at my words.

"I didn't want to frighten you like I did at the museum like I did on our first that. I'm trying my best to go slow with you so, let me know right now what you are ok with. That would help me immensely."

"That sounds like a plan. Let's on the couch while we talk ok?" I couldn't believe he wants to talk about what I'm ok with physically with him! No man before him cared to even here why I wasn't having sex with them before. Caius...Caius was different. I made us a fresh hot cup of apple cider that he had made just the day before for us to drink. This conversation could get heated or ugly real fast if the past was any inclination as to how he would react. I prayed that the Lord would be with me as I spoke to him and to help me be able to convey the importance of why I was sticking to my new rules. I walked back over into the living room to hand him his cup of apple cider.

"Thanks." He took the apple cider from my hand and patted the cushion next to him for me to sit on. I didn't. I moved to sit across from him on the couch to the side of him. If I was going to be able to get through this conversation I needed to make sure we had some physical distance between us. I needed to think clearly right now.

"Your welcome." I took a deep breath then started this hard conversation. "You asked me to tell you what my limits were?"

"Yes. I don't want to do anything that you deem inappropriate."

"Well, the most important thing is that I won't be having any form of sex until I am married." He nodded his head.

"The next one is that I can't be body to body with you in an embrace like what had just transpired. We can hug and play as you already know. Those acts of affection I'm learning are ok. I can handle those just fine."

"Yea, I did notice that you were ok with me hugging you now. What about kissing?"

"Kissing is ok chastely or French." I could see the relief followed by victory fly across his face. The poor man. I felt bad having to put him through all of this but, it was pivotal for me to stay to my rules.

"Anything else."

"I'm learning as we go along so, that's all I right now. For the sake of our relationship I hope that is it." I tell him with a laugh. He laughed with me then padded the cushion next to him again.

"Why are you so far away?"

"I wanted to make sure my mind was clear when I spoke to you about this. I didn't exactly know how this would play out. Most men haven't even gotten this far before they were out the door."

"Sareya, I'm not like those men. Matter of fact, I know for a fact that I am absolutely nothing like those jokers that you were with before. I want you to see that I am different and that I love you with all my heart."

"I can see that Caius. Trust me I can. You have no idea how happy you make me but, I can't shake the feeling that this isn't going to last. Like it's all too good to be true. What if you get tired of these rules and leave? What would happen to my heart then?"

"I can honestly tell you right now that I have no intention of leaving you in the near or distant future. You are far too fascinating for me to even think about leaving. Not to mention you are just so impossibly cute. Come here please. You're too far way." I got up to sit by Caius's side again. This is the spot I would be for the rest of my life if I didn't screw it up. It was where I wanted to be for the rest of my life.

"There. Doesn't that feel better?" He asked as he scooted me into his side. I laid my head on his chest so that I could listen to his heart beat. We sat in silence for a while just sitting on the couch together. After a couple of minutes, he sat up so that he could turn and look me in the face.

"I thought about your rules Sareya. I don't see why I can't abide by them for you. I know what you've been through and the last thing I want is scare you away or disrespect you. You don't have to worry about me pressuring you or trying to get you to do something that you don't want to do. So, don't worry ok." He kissed my forehead then laid me back down on his chest. This man was unbelievable.

"Thank you, Caius. I appreciate everything your saying and all the hard work you're going to put into this. I couldn't have asked for a better man than you to do it."

"I value you highly Sareya. Believe it or not you have saved me from myself. It's because of you I can see a new storyline in my life when I thought my story was already written. You basically did a rewrite and I am very excited about the results."

"For me; you are finishing the book of my life when I thought there was nothing left about me to even be written. I'm excited to see what each new chapter of my life has in store. I get the feeling with you it'll be a lot of fun." He smiled from ear to ear. After 15 minutes I looked at the clock and saw that it was almost 8:00 pm. I decided to turn the TV on, so we could watch some shows curled up on the couch.

"You want to watch some TV huh?"

"Yea, I need to catch up on my show New Girl." I announced as I turned on the latest episode. I sat back in my spot more comfortably with my legs over his and my back on the armrest.

"Comfortable?" He asked teasingly.

"Very. Have you watched this show before?" I admitted.

"I can't say that I have. From what you've told me I bet this is a comedy isn't it?"

"You would be correct with that statement."

The show began so, I stopped talking to him after that. He seemed to like the show too. He watched it with me, asked questions. He even asked me to remind him when the next episode came on.

"Do you have cable in your apartment?" I asked him while selecting the next show on my DVR to watch.

"Yep. When I get home, I will make sure to set my DVR as soon as I step inside the door."

"Wouldn't that be difficult to do since you won't have the remote in your hand to set the DVR yet?"

"Oh, Sareya!" He yelled and immediately started tickling me. I hated being tickled but for some reason when he did it everything was ok. I didn't mind it at all. It was another form of affection that I could handle so, I welcomed it.

"Stop…. tickling" I couldn't even get the words out of my mouth. Instead I rolled to the floor and tried to crawl to safety.

"Oh no you don't." He said cheerfully. He followed me onto the floor and tackled on the area rug. I couldn't get away if I wanted to. He was bigger than me and just as deftly. He had my defenses overcome within seconds and before I knew it I was rolling around the floor in laughter. Somehow, I managed to break away from him and get to the other side of the living without any further problem. I took a moment to catch my breath while he remained in his current spot.

"Please don't tickle me anymore." I begged breathlessly. I staggered off the floor and sat in a nearby chair. Caius stood up walked over to the chair I was sitting in. He was still chuckling to himself about something but, I didn't know what it was for. Reaching out he took my hair in his hands and fluffed my hair back out for me. Apparently, my hair had become smooshed during one of his tickling attacks.

"Thank you. I didn't know it was looking like that."

"No problem." He said and sat down at my feet. He laid his head on my lap to rest while he caught his breath. Feeling hot and sweaty I didn't want to touch him too much. Just in case I smelled bad. It was fun though. I couldn't believe he attacked me with a tickle attack. It was fun.

"What made you want to tickle me so much?"

"I wanted to hear your laugh." He said this to me so easily you would've thought it was a normal occurrence to say that to me. He must really feel comfortable with me.

"I see. Why was that?" I was cheesin so much I could hardly stand it. All he wanted to hear me laugh.

"Hmmm. The better question would be why not?" He exclaimed.

"Touché`." Agreeing with that statement wasn't wrong at all.

"Your lap is very comfortable by the way. Do you specialize in lap therapy?"

"Lap Therapy?"

"Yea, I heard it's something that only women have that allows men and children the ability to fall asleep at a moment notice from pure comfort."

"Are you saying that I have this ability?"

"I would say so. If I stay here for another minute or so I'm pretty sure I will fall asleep."

I giggled. I admit that I was enjoying feeling him laying on my lap. I touched his head and felt how warm it felt under my touch. That was a huge feat considering that I was burning up from running away from him seconds not too long ago. His bald head felt so smooth and the color was such an even color. I learned that he had Alopecia when we were talking during dinner last night so, he doesn't grow any hair. I found that to be very refreshing. I never was a fan of facial hair or hairy men to tell the truth. To find out that he didn't grow any hair at all was great news for me to hear.

"Are you asleep yet?"

"Nope. I'm ¾ of the way there though."

"Would you like me to get you a blanket?"

Suddenly, he sat up abruptly. A look of alarm was evident on his face from what I had just asked him.

"Sareya, I told you that I would abide by the rules so, staying the night wouldn't be good idea."

I laughed at him. I couldn't help it. He looked so cute with that look on his face. I just had to poke fun at him.

"I was just kidding Caius. I wasn't really going to let you sleep in my lap. I know having you stay the night would not be a great idea."

"Have you ever been to the zoo? He stared at me carefully as he carefully chose his next words. I loved the fact that you could tell that he was thinking.

"Huh?"

"So. you know you shouldn't dangle meat in front of a hungry lion, right?"

I cracked up laughing. "Alright, I got it. I won't joke like that again." I promised.

He seemed sufficed with that then laid his head back down on my lap.

"Shall we move to the couch so; we can see the tv though? I wasn't done watching the tv when you attacked me."

"That's fine. Here let me help you out." He stood up and gingerly carried me back over the couch. He sat me down gently and plopped himself right next to me. The motion made me bounce off the cushion and he caught coming back down. He laid me back down on his chest then rested his head on the top of my head. Rubbing my arms absentmindedly while we watched TV brought an end to the 3$^{rd}$ date that we have had. Snuggled up on the couch was the perfect way to end the all-day date that we had just had. I couldn't wat till we had another way.

# 17
## CHAPTER

I awoke refreshed and ready to start my first day at work for the week. This past weekend had been a blast. Even though Caius and I had planned to only have a dinner date where we cooked together on Saturday, we ended up going out all day for another date on Sunday. It was the best weekend of my life. He had heard some more about my past and just like from the beginning he wasn't fazed. He declared once again that he wanted to be with me. I was beginning to think that there would be nothing that I could've said to change his mind even if I wanted to. The drive to work was nice on another bright sunny mild winter day. It wasn't currently raining or snowing and to makes matters even better there wasn't any in the forecast for the next week either. Traffic was clear all the way to the hospital. I was so thankful for that. I parked in my designated spot in the parking garage and made way into the doors to the hospital.

Once I was inside I felt like I was seeing couples everywhere around me. I heard that this happened when you started seeing someone but, I didn't think that it was true. On my way up to my department I counted 10 couples that I saw just from the main entrance door all the way to the elevator. This is ridiculous I thought to myself when I stepped off the elevator.

"Well, good morning Sunshine!" Shania yelled from the hallway.

"Good Morning Shania!" I yelled back at her.

"Woah, are you awake this morning? Are you happy this morning?"

"It would seem so." I proclaimed as I walked past her into the breakroom to make my daily morning tea for work.

"I am shocked and appalled! Shocked and appalled I tell you." She said following me into the breakroom.

"Well, I am. How are you this morning? Did you do anything on Sunday?"

"Nope. I just slept in after hanging out all night with Luann."

"I understand that completely." I agreed. I finished making my tea and started heading toward my office. She followed me silently till we shut the door behind us in my office. I sat down in my chair, turned on my computer, and set my jacket and purse in my desk drawer. Shania was patiently waiting sitting across from my desk in one of the red chairs.

"Are you going to tell me how your date went?" She asked impatiently.

"Oh, I'm sorry I forgot."

"You forgot? How could you forget that? It just happened yesterday!" She exclaimed.

"I was focused on just getting to work when I got here. I wasn't thinking about my dates like that.

Shaking her head out of frustration she continued to ask me more detailed questions.

"I don't buy it for a minute that you forgot all about your dates that just happened in the last two days. That's just ludicrous. Don't try to lie to me about that." She said in her trademark sassy tone.

"Ok. Fine. I was thinking about it but, I was trying to get my head in the game after the weekend that we had."

"Cool. Now what happened on your date yesterday?"

"Well, he took me to IHOP for breakfast and I got their New York City cheesecake pancakes with scrambled eggs and turkey bacon."

"Yea, IHOP has great food." She nodded aggressively.

"After breakfast he took me to the theatre to see a movie.

"What did you see? A drama? A Romance movie?"

"Actually, we went and saw a musical and it was great."

"Oh…ok."

"Then after that we walked a couple blocks down to an ice cream shop that he wanted to take me to. One the way you know how there are so many different shops that sell clothes, shoes, etc. right?"

"Yes."

"Well, there a dress on a mannequin right in the stores window."

"It was such a beautiful dress that I couldn't think of anything but, trying the dress on."

"Oh Girl, I've been there."

"Exactly, you know what I'm sorry. We went into the store to try it on and would you know that he bought it for me?"

"What! He did. Get out!"

"No, he really did. He even said that we need to find an event, so you can wear it."

"Oh wow. Do you have a picture of it?" I took out my phone and showed it to her. I took a picture of it after Caius went home last night.

"OOOOOOOO Girl! That dress looks hot on you!"

"Thanks." I said shyly.

"You really are. I see why he wants to create an event somewhere just, so you wear that dress."

"Yea, I really appreciate him buying it for me and I found it difficult to accept him paying for me for a little bit."

"Why would you worry about that. Do you know how many women out there wish they had a man that had it all together in their lives. Shoot, at least men that keep a stable job."

"Ok. You have a point."

"I know that you don't want a man to do everything for you but, there's nothing wrong with being pampered and treated like a queen by him. That's how men are supposed to treat their wives. Unlike some people I know who even like to buy me anything on Valentine's day or your birthday because they feel it's just a holiday that was made up by Hallmark."

I started to feel tension in the air rising from Shania as she continued to vent about this mystery guy. I decided to interrupt he for the time being.

"Alright, I know what you're saying. I should allow him to treat me special because, I am special."

"Bingo. Besides, would you really be thinking about dating him if he didn't pay for your dates and stuff?"

"Good point as always Shania. I wouldn't pay him any attention if he couldn't afford to take me out on a date. I promised myself that I deserved better and that I wasn't going to settle for less than I was worth."

"Testify girl! Testify!" Before I realized it, she started jumping up and down in the office.

"Ok. Shania calm down. I heard you. I will let that go about him buying things for me."

"Good. I don't want to hear you talk about foolishness like that again. You have a good man and you are going to sit here and complain about him buying you things. Just when you thought you heard it all." She said as she stood to walk out of my office. She was shaking her head when he walked out the door still mumbling to herself. I guess I really annoyed her because she didn't even ask me to finish telling her about the date. I guess I would just tell her at lunchtime.

I looked at my computer and clicked on my office email icon. I checked it and saw that there was an email from Eli saying there was a meeting today at 10 am about a new hospital policy that they wanted to go over and vote on. I emailed him back letting him know that I would be there and began to check on my other emails.

At 9:45 am my alarm went off on my computer to let me know it was time for me to wrap up whatever I was doing so, that I could be there on time for the meeting. I was composing an email when Eli walked through the door.

"Morning Sareya."

"Morning Eli. How are you?"

"I'm good. I heard you went on another date with your new boyfriend this past weekend."

Yea, I did." I said gleefully.

"It went well I take it?" He said as he leaned on my office wall.

"It surely did go well." I didn't dare tell him what God told me about Caius. One thing I knew for sure was that he wouldn't believe me if I told him. He would think I came up with this in my imagination since I used to say that whoever I was dating was the one back then. I pretty much beat that statement like a dead horse.

"He seems promising huh? The look on your face suggests that. Anyone could tell looking at you." He pointed out.

"He makes me so happy. It makes sense that he would make me express my emotions on my face."

"I can honestly say that you look stress free and happier. That says a lot considering that today is Friday."

"I'm glad that you noticed that. If you noticed that then others must see it too. I was told growing up that I needed to look for a man that made me a better person, happy, and relaxed all at the same time. He does just that."

Eli said nothing else to me but, grinned at me.

I got my tablet and followed him out to the hallway so, we could make the meeting on time.

"Are you upset about something?" I inquired.

"Nope. I was just remembering when we were younger how I hit on you and you immediately turned me down."

I remember it going over more smoothly than that but, what made you think of that?"

He stopped walking toward the elevators and pulled me into the breakroom. Now nobody was in there so, we were safe to talk without anyone over hearing.

"I asked because I've seen you with the same type of joker over and over. You deserve to be with someone that sees how special you are and treats you right. I guess I always just wondered how come you never considered me?"

"I never wanted to ruin our friendship if we had dated. I wanted you to find someone that was head over heels I love with you. You deserved that too."

He hung his head down for a moment and then raised it back up to look at me.

"That's answer is okay with me. I just had to know. Just so you know though I will always look out for you. I don't ever want you to go through what you went through before. If you ever need me just contact me ok?

"Ok."

Work went by fast and before I knew it was time to go home. I was very happy that the meeting we had in the morning was not an extensive meeting. I grabbed my things and headed home amongst the rush hour traffic. The sun was gone and there were clouds in the sky. The weather report called for rain but, nothing that would cause any accidents apparently. I did notice that it was very windy outside though. I drove on the highway heading toward my house and after eight minutes I saw my exit to get off.

I drove off the exit ramp and made a right to head to my house. I lived in a subdivision so, it was a quieter and peaceful area compared to the people who lived downtown amidst the nightlife. If you lived down, there it would be noise galore and I didn't want to live amid all of that.

When I got close to my garage I pushed the button the sun visor. The door silently rumbled to life and raised itself to the top of the garage. I pulled into my garage and once I was all the way inside I pushed the button again for it to come back down. I got out of my car as it was coming down and I heard the wind starting to pick up outside. Unlocking my interior garage door that leads to the kitchen I took my time walking into the house. It sounded so quiet and empty. I walked into my bedroom and once again noticed just how quiet it really was.

"Wow, I had Caius in my house for the weekend and now it seems so quiet without him here. It feels so empty without him here too. I miss him." I thought to myself. I decided to call him after I took a shower and change my clothes. I walked into the bathroom and turned on my shower. At the sink I took my hairstyle down and decided to just leave my hair in its natural curly state for the rest of the day. It would look like an afro but in its natural curl pattern with it not picked out. After taking my hair down I jumped in the shower and with 10 minutes I was out of the shower and dressed in my walk-in closet. I grabbed my phone off the bed.

I immediately saw that Luann had called me while I was in the shower. I called her back and she answered on the first ring.

"Hey Girl! How did your date go yesterday?"

'It was great. I had a fun time with him yesterday. He even bought me a dress."

"He did?" I couldn't believe I said that like it was a normal occurrence. I guess what Shania said was really taken to heart.

"Yep. We went to IHOP first for breakfast then we went to see a movie together. We saw a musical and it was wonderful. We then walked a couple of blocks to go get some ice cream. On the way we walked passed a store that had a beautiful red dress in the window.

"Girl for real!? You did all of that and even got to get a beautiful red dress? Man, I'm jealous of you."

"That's what Shania said. I originally had an issue with him buying me things but, Shania helped me see that it was a waste of my time."

"Heck yea it is! You know how many women wish that their men would buy them something. Shoot! Many of them wish that they would just have a man let alone one with a job."

"I get it. I should appreciate the fact that the man not only has a job but, that he also wants to buy you things."

"Girl, Yes! Last time I checked you've never had a man with all of that before have you?"

"No. I haven't. That's why it feels so weird to have a man buy me something now. I've gotten used to doing things and buying things on my own."

"There's nothing wrong with a man buying you things to show his token of love for you. I beg you please don't ruin this for me. Please don't ruin this for any of us really. Right now, I'm living my life vicariously through you so, don't mess this up."

"Man, no pressure." Luann was laying it on thick. I didn't know that she was counting on me so much. I didn't know that she was looking at me to show her what true love looks like. That made me see just how serious to was not only for me but for her as well.

"I don't mean to say it that way. I want you to understand that the man you have is a great one."

"You haven't even gotten to know him yet. How can you be so sure that you like him already?"

"It's because I see the positive changes he's made in you. In such a short period of time you have gone out on dates, spoken positively about men, and took the time to talk to us about what is happening to you. You didn't bother to do that after college. It's been three years before you wanted to share what was happening in your life with me. I can't feel anything else for the man but, happiness. I have a really good feeling about him."

"I do too. He is the best man that I have ever met."

We talked for a little bit longer then promised to talk to each other tomorrow. She was right about the positive changes he made in me. Even I couldn't deny that fact. I was able to hold hands with him, kiss him, and dance with him without wanting to do something inappropriate. That meant so much to me. He has opened a door to a world I didn't think that I could ever walk through. I thought it was impossible for me but, it wasn't impossible for God. He gave me this man to share my life with. I didn't want to do anything to ruin it. At least consciously.

# 18
## CHAPTER

I'd just gotten home from work and gotten off the phone with Luann when I decided to watch some TV. I watched a couple episodes of my favorite show while I ate the leftovers of the lasagna that Caius made for me. Even with it being heated back up it still tasted delicious. Before I knew it, I was missing him. I checked my phone to see if he'd called and saw that Caius had called a couple of minutes ago. I must've been rinsing off the dishes when he called. He must've just gotten home from work. I called him back and hoped that he would answer the phone on the first ring. Even though it had been a couple of minutes since he called I didn't think that he would be that far away from his phone. The phone rang a total of three times when he finally answered the phone.

"Hi Sareya. How are you today? He asked.

"I'm doing good" I told him.

"How was your day to day?"

"It was to be expected working in my line of work. How was yours?"

"Our day went much better than it had been. That was because we didn't have any person that came to teach us something beneficial anymore."

"I'm glad that you don't have those workshops anymore. You were calling me every day after work to complain about the way they were teaching you."

"I know you went a through a lot for me and I am forever grateful for that. It was rough having to deal with those seminars. It was really exhausting."

"I can only imagine. When we switched to another EMR program we had someone come out and it lasted for almost two months."

"Two months. I can't imagine going through something like that for so long."

"It wasn't so bad. The teacher we had was very nice. She was also very great as a teacher."

"I'm glad you got a good one. I wouldn't wish that person on my worst enemy."

I couldn't stop laughing. He was so silly I couldn't believe it. It must have really been a bad set of seminars.

"Are you guys going to be implementing the new security system at your job or are you guys selling it?"

"We are going to use it. The company decided to start creating new deals with other medical groups. To do that we needed to upgrade the software program that we were currently using."

"Oh. So, you guys only had a couple of deals at the time."

"We had about…. well sorta. I guess the president wanted to expand and wanted to pick up a few more contracts."

"Were the people on board with that?"

"Yes. It meant a raise and some even got promoted. The company has a great track record of taking care of their employees as well as a great benefits package."

"That's why you applied there right after school huh?"

"Yep. I interned there, and they liked me a lot. They asked me to apply there so, I did. Within a couple of days, I was a full fledge employee and I had just attended my graduation."

"You didn't ask to officially start a couple of weeks after graduation?"

"I know I did. I wanted a break after all these years of studying."

"Nope. I was ready to get out of my parent's house so, I couldn't wait to save up enough to get my own place."

"Well, you have a good point." I giggled.

"I've been there now for almost a year and I don't regret my decision. It's close to my job, it has great benefits, and the pay is very good."

"That's all that matters in the long run I guess huh?"

"That and job fulfillment."

"That's very true!" We laughed together for a couple of minutes. I laid on my bed to help catch my breath after laughing so hard.

"What plans do you have this evening?"

"I'm just going to lay around and relax. After the long weekend I had I don't want to do anything else right now."

"Oh, you had a looooonnnnnnnnggggg weekend huh?"

I giggled to myself. "It was a long weekend but, it wasn't that long. I had a great time. I can't wait to do it again but, for tonight I just want to lay around and do nothing else."

"I really tired you out did I? We just had too much fun it seems." He chuckled.

"Well, not exactly. There was a meeting today and it was only supposed to last for 30 minutes. However, it lasted for over an hour and it was unnecessary. I told them that the policy they wanted to implement wasn't necessary but, they insisted anyway. It was like they wanted to anger the employees or something. At least that's how it felt. In the end they decided to go without the change in the policy. I felt that it was better the way it was. It would only cause more and further issues if they decided to go with it. Thankfully in the end they chose to keep it the way it was."

"Sometimes it takes a strong person to say there's nothing wrong with what we have already. I've seen it myself where too many are in the pot and they ruin the flavor of the food. If it's going to destroy employee morale, then they should just leave it alone. If it ain't broke don't fix it."

"Exactly! I don't know where it came from in the first place that it needed to be changed."

"Shoot, who knows. It was probably just one person who it didn't benefit. Especially if they are troublemakers to begin with."

"That's very true. It's amazing how one person can cause such a ruckus yet the person who doesn't cause any problems gets in trouble at times."

"Your preaching to the choir on that one. That's why it's best if you just let God take the lead."

"That's very true. You are a very wise man Caius."

"You think so huh? I need to call my parents and let them know what you just said."

"Man, they must not give you much credit, do they?"

"They do when credit is due but, things like this are hard to prove unless they are there to witness it."

"My parents are like that too. It's just how parents are I guess. You are not alone."

"Good. I now have someone to help me fight in this war of attrition.

"Your right about that. We need all the help we can get right?"

"Exactly."

I rolled onto my belly to get more comfortable. Talking to Caius has proven to be an eventful experience every single time we have spoken. I was beginning to look forward to it every night when he would call to talk to me. Trusting him didn't come that easy to me though. Trusting him has been a big deal for me. I know that I can't let my past overtake the present as easy as that can be. It's simple to tell a man that you don't want him around because you don't trust him. If he's not around he can't hurt me and if he can't hurt me then I'm safe. However, the problem with that is you find yourself lonely. In any relationship it's give and take. In every relationship it takes work to sustain it. If you find that you don't have the patience or the time to dedicate to it, then it's best that you don't date anyone. For me that's not true. I have the time and the patience. I just didn't want to waste time on any man that I wasn't supposed to be with. I know women who want a relationship but, don't seem to understand that to have one you have to trust him first. They felt that it was ok to never trust a man in a relationship. The truth is you're only going to add more stress and pain by thinking that way. I decided to live for tomorrow and to be happy for once in my life. The road I took wasn't the right one before but, now I was finally on the right track.

"On second thought. Would you like to come over?" It was quiet for maybe two seconds before he responded. I heard rustling going on in the background. I think I also heard him grab a set of keys.

"I thought you'd never ask. I'll be there in 15 minutes."

"I can't wait."